Also By Dannika

THE MAGERI SERIES
Sterling
Twist
Impulse
Gravity
Shine
The Gift (Novella)

NOVELLAS
Closer

THE SEVEN SERIES
Seven Years
Six Months
Five Weeks
Four Days
Three Hours
Two Minutes
One Second
Winter Moon (Novella)

SEVEN WORLD
Charming

Dear Reader

If you have not read the Seven series, this novella takes place after the final book. Please begin with *Seven Years*, book one in the Seven series.

I'd like to dedicate this novella to my pack. Your unwavering love for these characters continues to inspire me. Thank you for taking the journey and opening your hearts to these stories.

CHAPTER 1

Lexi and Austin

"TRAVIS, HOLD STILL," LEXI CHIDED as she struggled to put on his other sneaker.

"No!"

No was her little boy's favorite word. Travis was sixteen months and a handful, just like his father. Same alpha spirit, same icy blue eyes, same stubborn streak. The only characteristics that Travis had inherited from Lexi were her sense of humor and signature laugh.

Travis giggled when he flipped onto his stomach. He quickly scrambled to his feet and squawked as he scampered down the hall toward the kitchen. Lexi erupted with laughter because when Travis ran, he looked like a drunken old man. Whenever he tripped and fell, which was often, he rarely cried. Fortitude was a common trait among alpha children.

Lexi remained seated on the floor, her gaze fixed on the crackling fire in the hearth. The staircase wall on the left made it a cozy place to sit. Usually they kept the space open to give everyone access to the guest bathroom beneath the stairs, but in the winter they'd drag the sofa and chairs from the right side of the room and arrange them around the fireplace where there weren't any drafts. The staircase wall boxed in the heat, and the firelight danced sublimely off the wood floors.

While they hadn't put up a Christmas tree this year, a few of her packmates had decorated the house with simple adornments. A garland on the mantel, a few white lights strewn around the windows and up the staircase, and a wicker basket filled with scented pinecones in the sitting room up front. The holidays had snuck up on them, and it wasn't until the last minute that Lexi realized they didn't have a Christmas tree.

"Hold on, little man," Austin boomed from the hall.

Travis squealed with delight when Austin lifted him into his arms.

"Where's your shoe? Is your mama trying to dress you again? Didn't you tell her that the Coles are wild men who don't wear shoes?" He gave Lexi a playful wink and strode around the sofa.

Travis wrapped his arms around his daddy's neck. Sometimes it brought tears to her eyes to see that bond between them. She had never known a father's love, so watching Austin's face light up each time he laid eyes on Travis filled her heart with unspeakable joy.

Lexi tapped the little shoe against the red-and-brown area rug. "Austin, he can't run around barefoot."

"Why not? We do."

"If we didn't, we'd track in dirt. It's too cold, and what if he steps on something sharp?"

Austin took the shoe from her hand and sat down in the leather chair with Travis in his lap. "Let's see your foot, little man. Show me what a big boy you are."

Travis always wanted to impress his daddy, so he lifted his leg and allowed Austin to slip on the sneaker. Lexi took a mental picture to capture it in her memory. She loved the small moments they shared, which were often eclipsed by first words, first steps, and birthdays. Austin was never more handsome to Lexi than when he was holding his son.

"Kitty!" Travis pointed his chubby little finger at the cat entering the room.

Sparty strutted over and sat on the hearth, his soot-colored fur giving him a shadowy appearance. When his pink tongue poked out, Travis giggled and squirmed until Austin set him on the floor to chase the cat around.

On days when the pack was home and scattered throughout the house, everyone watched Travis. Packs believed that each member of the family was responsible for raising a child, and that was how they created a bond. Lexi never felt overwhelmed with being a new mom, especially with her mother around, who was still basking in the afterglow of grandmotherhood. Lynn would sing to Travis, take him for long walks on the property, and loved reading him stories.

Lexi reclined on her back, one arm folded beneath her head. "How much more snow are we supposed to get?"

Austin leaned back and ran a hand through his dark hair. "Eight inches."

"Mmm, now *that's* what I like to hear," Naya purred as she entered the room with impeccable timing.

Naya loved a good innuendo.

Lexi watched her saunter into the front study where Travis had gone. Wheeler was in there—kicked back in a chair and no doubt trying to get Travis to eat a piece of dried-up jerky. Their interactions were always hilarious since Travis's vocabulary was limited. He couldn't pronounce Wheeler's name correctly, so he just called him Wheels.

Austin scooted out of his chair and crawled next to her. He nudged his right leg between her thighs and brushed his lips against the soft curve of her neck. Everything about it felt so damn right: his musky scent, his experienced hand caressing her breasts, his lips traveling down to her shoulder. Austin's body heat rivaled any fire, so in the winter she often slept naked, all pressed up against him.

"Did someone wrap the faucets outside?"

"You worry too much," he murmured against her neck.

She replied in honeyed tones. "No big deal. Just the snowstorm of the century."

"I thought you liked snow."

She nibbled on his earlobe. "I like four inches, but we've

already had seven. This is Texas, not Ontario. When have we ever had this much snow?"

Lexi gasped when he rocked his hips against her, his fingers crawling beneath her shirt and pinching her nipple. Her body tingled and came alive, wanting more—needing more.

"Let's cancel Christmas and make babies," he suggested, kissing her neck more insistently, his whiskers scratching against her skin.

"There's not much to cancel."

Austin rolled onto his side and rested his head in the palm of his hand. "I know we waited until the last minute to do things, but it'll be fine."

"I know. I just wish we would have bought a plastic tree before they sold out."

Denver strode in and plopped on the sofa. "Plastic?" He dipped his spoon into a can of SpaghettiOs. "The Weston pack doesn't do plastic."

Lexi sat up. "Nobody complained about our old plastic tree. If it hadn't caught fire last year—"

"That tree burning down was a sign." He waved his spoon, and a dollop of sauce fell on his bare chest. "Do you want a real donut or a fake? A real mate or a plastic one?"

"Depends on the speed settings," Naya said, rushing toward the kitchen.

"You're a pervy little panther," he yelled over his shoulder.

Lexi stared at the empty corner. Everyone had forgotten

about last year's fire until a few days ago. By that point, it was too late to bother with a tree, so everyone agreed on not decking the halls this year. The Cole brothers behaved as if they couldn't care less about decorating for the holidays.

But that wasn't entirely true.

It hadn't escaped her attention how they were the ones who took the lights out of the box and volunteered to string them up outside the house. Christmas had never been a big deal for the Coles—not the way people celebrated it nowadays. The brothers would grumble about how the spirit of Christmas was dead and the holidays were all about commercialism and profit. But when the lights were aglow, their eyes twinkled. That kind of magic was worth every penny, so it was disheartening to see that this year everyone seemed okay without a tree. What was next? No lights? No presents?

Lexi stripped her eyes away from the empty corner and watched the flames leaping and dancing in the hearth.

"Are you going to sulk all day?" Denver asked. After another bite of his pasta, he set the can down and stood up. "Fine. You talked me into it. I'll go get a stinkin' tree."

The way he bounced on his toes belied his reluctant words. Lexi had brought up the tree that morning, but everyone had an excuse about the snow. Since she wasn't badgering anyone about it, they hadn't taken her seriously. But no one liked seeing a female unhappy, and Denver must have hit his limit.

"I don't see why we can't chop down a tree from out back," Austin suggested. "We've got an axe."

Lexi drummed her fingers on the floor. "Those aren't Christmas trees. It'll wind up looking like the Charlie Brown tree if you try to hang an ornament from a baby maple. They're probably all sold out of real ones anyhow." She looked up at Denver, suddenly feeling a smidge of guilt for putting him out. "Why don't you just go to Walmart and—"

"Over my dead body," Denver retorted. "You're a bag of nuts if you think I'm going in that madhouse the day before Christmas. Anyhow, they sold out. Remember? There's a tree farm not too far from here where you can go cut down your own."

"Sounds like a big-boy job." Wheeler swaggered into the room and gave him a once-over. "You can't even cut your own steak."

Denver held up his middle finger. "Shut it."

Wheeler gnawed on a piece of jerky, his hair disheveled and sticking out in every direction. "Don't worry, Lexi. I'll babysit dickhead here. I need to stretch my legs and get out of the house anyway."

Denver yanked the jerky out of Wheeler's mouth and stalked toward the front door. "Then maybe you need to stretch your legs to the cat box and clean it out. I'll be warming up the truck." He put on his white down coat with a NASA emblem on it and glanced up the stairs. "Wanna go for a ride, Peanut?"

Maizy came halfway down the stairs and leaned over the handrail. She had her blond hair pulled up in a ponytail. "Where are you going?"

"To saw down a tree."

"Have fun with that!" she said, jogging back upstairs.

"You're going on my naughty list!" Still shirtless, Denver zipped up his coat and searched through the shoe pile.

Lexi smiled. The idea of having a real tree made her a little giddy, and suddenly she wanted to bake a pie.

Wheeler grabbed his leather jacket from the closet. "You look like the Stay Puft Marshmallow Man from that movie."

Denver ran his fingers down his coat and admired it. "It's vintage, but you wouldn't know anything about style."

"Thank the fuck for that. Let's go, Puffy."

Austin scooted behind Lexi and wrapped his strong arms around her. "See, Ladybug? Everything's going to work out the way it always does. Even without a tree, we've still got the pack, and that's all that matters."

"I know. I just want traditions that don't always involve a barbecue."

Travis shrieked from the study, and they listened to the sound of his little feet stomping across the living room.

"Come back here, little baby," Naya sang. "Auntie Naya's going to tickle you!"

Austin rocked with laughter when Travis disappeared in the kitchen and let out a silly laugh.

Lexi's laugh.

She leaned against Austin and smiled. "Sounds like his little wolf knows a panther is chasing him."

"Hmm. Maybe I should teach him not to run from anyone."

"Not everything has to be a lesson, Daddy Packmaster. Let him play."

Travis was just a baby, but Lexi was learning just how differently Shifter children were raised from human ones. Especially alphas. Austin was always cognizant of how Travis reacted to the world around him, and every situation became an opportunity to groom him as an alpha. Luckily, Jericho's alpha twins were much older. Otherwise there could have been a lot of friction in the house with their wolf spirits fighting for rank. Even though the kids wouldn't go through their first change until later in life, those animal instincts were embedded in their DNA.

Lynn entered the room with two steaming cups of hot apple cider. "You two kids drink these before they get cold," she said, setting the mugs on an end table before returning to the kitchen.

Austin kissed Lexi's temple. "I love the way she still calls us kids. It takes me back."

Lexi pulled away and got on all fours to get her drink. "Oh? Does it take you back to when you used to pluck the eyes out of my stuffed animals?"

He slapped her behind playfully.

"Mmm, do that again and we might have to cancel Christmas after all," she purred, tingles roaring. When she glanced over her shoulder at him and shook her ass, Austin's black pupils swallowed up all that icy blue. That man could make her toes curl every single time. His alpha energy hummed against her skin as he looked at her with a fervent gaze.

Austin gripped the waistband of her jeans and bit one of her cheeks. "That cider won't keep you half as warm as I will."

"We'll see about that."

He gave her a wolfish grin. "Challenge accepted."

CHAPTER 2

April and Reno

"I SHOULDN'T HAVE WAITED UNTIL THE last minute to buy gifts." April sulked, staring at the barren makeup aisle at Walgreens. The good stuff was already gone thanks to a recent holiday sale.

Reno held up a bottle of pink nail polish. "How 'bout this?"

April gave it a cursory glance and returned her attention to the top shelf. "Pink isn't Mel's style. She's going through that teen phase where she wants to be different. She's not really into nail polish, but I thought I might find a wild color. The only ones left are the shades that no one likes."

What made the situation worse was the weather. After the slippery drive to the store, they agreed not to venture anywhere else. Especially since Reno had borrowed Austin's Dodge Challenger. April was forced to do all her last-minute shopping at the drugstore—her karmic reward for procrastinating.

Reno's wet boots squeaked against the floor as he circled

behind her and kissed the top of her blond head. "She'll like whatever you get her, princess."

April smiled up at him. Reno was six foot three and built like a soldier. Even though he was over a hundred, he looked like a man in his late thirties. Now that she'd become a Mage, they finally appeared the same age. April loved everything about her man, especially when she could make that tough guy smile. He winked, amusement dancing in those dark brown eyes, and swaggered to the back of the store.

April tugged on the ends of her short hair and resumed scanning the shelves.

The twins were into hunting and fishing, so she'd ordered fishing poles for them a few months ago. They liked the outdoors, and ever since the war, they'd spent more time camping in the woods. Reno said their alpha nature was telling them to brush up on their survival instincts—something they'd need in order to effectively lead a pack one day.

But Mel, she was another story. Since Izzy was giving her a collection of beads and scrap material for designing clothes, April didn't want to eclipse her gift with something similar. She figured an idea would come to her eventually, but now it was the eleventh hour, and she still didn't have a clue.

At least she'd taken care of Reno.

Last month, April remembered a box of tools Reno had been eyeing earlier that year. His were rusty antiques, and some were missing. Even though they rarely exchanged gifts, April purchased the tools on the sly. He enjoyed working on his bike and fixing things around the house. Maybe it wasn't the most extravagant gift she could have come up with, but Reno was too cheap with himself. He deserved something special.

She scanned the bottom row and spotted crackle nail polish. Was that still in fashion? She lifted the black bottle and then snatched up a few of the less horrific shades of pink for a base coat.

"I can't just get her nail polish," she muttered, staring into the empty basket. If only Mel was into reading. April knew all the best books, but there weren't many avid readers living in the Weston pack.

She spun around and crashed into a guy. "Holy smokes!"

April lost her balance and almost careened into a shelf before the man clutched her arms. "Whoa," he said with a deep chuckle. "Slow down there."

She peered up at the older man. His salt-and-pepper beard was mostly salt, and his blue eyes twinkled like crystal waters beneath a summer sky.

April grimaced when a button popped off his red flannel shirt from where her fists were grasping. She finally untangled her legs and stood up straight. "I'm sorry about that."

"I'm not." He continued smiling blithely at her, and that's when she sensed he was Breed.

Since April had become a Mage, she'd developed the ability

to tell humans apart from Breed by their energy. Though what exactly they were remained a mystery.

The man glanced in her basket. "Last-minute shopping?" He showed off his empty basket. "Me too. Got any ideas for what to get an ornery old woman who never leaves the house?"

"Cable?"

He chortled. "I got her a dish last year. We promised no gifts, but you know how that goes," he said with a friendly wink.

April fiddled with a beaded bracelet around her wrist. "I'm trying to find something for my niece. She just turned seventeen."

The man stroked his beard. "That doesn't seem too challenging."

"You don't know Melody. She's an archer who likes to sew. I can't get her anything to do with sewing since her mother is taking care of that." April touched the man's arm. "I'm sorry to bore you. I'll let you get back to your shopping."

"Not at all," he replied, his voice resonant and warm. "I don't get out much. It's good to talk to someone besides the wife. You strike me as a lovely person, and I'm sure your niece will like whatever you give her." He held up one finger, his cheeks rosy. "Just remember, it's the thought that counts."

April glanced in her basket. "This seems pretty thoughtless. A few cheap bottles of polish—not even something she wants. Holidays are so much easier when the kids are little. Now that she's all grown up, I want to put more thought into her gifts. Serves me right for waiting until the last minute."

Her spirit sagged along with her shoulders as a jovial Christmas song played on the intercom. Sure, she could buy a gift card, but that was about as exciting as giving her a wad of cash.

The man circled his finger over a loose thread where his button once was. "Let me give you a piece of advice," he began. "Don't waste precious time fretting over the things that don't really matter. Love, health, happiness—those things matter. Gifts under the tree? Not so much. The fates will give us what we've earned. Merry Christmas, young one."

A bell jingled when he disappeared around the corner.

The store was bustling with shoppers wrapped up in winter coats and long scarves, and their eyes told the story that they were all in the same predicament. A few had prescriptions to fill, but the vast majority wandered the aisles like postapocalyptic survivors in search of supplies.

April hurried to the back to see if there was anything good she'd overlooked, but the only thing she found were first aid supplies and clearance items. "Gee, thanks, Aunt April. I always wanted a tube of ointment."

"Mmm, I could use some ointment," Reno murmured from behind.

April spun around. "Ointment and lube are not the same."

She wrinkled her nose. "Why do you smell like… Exactly what *is* that smell?"

He organized a few boxes of bandages on the shelf. "Ran into an older lady who couldn't decide which lotion she wanted to give her husband, so she rubbed it all over my neck and took a whiff."

April bubbled with laughter and gripped the opening of his leather jacket. "You're such a nice guy. That's why I fell in love with you."

"I thought it was my six-pack." His eyes glittered with amusement as he looked down at her with pure adoration in those coffee-brown eyes. Reno was a big guy with a tough demeanor, but he had a heart of gold beneath that macho exterior. He could melt her heart with a single glance, and he was thoughtful in ways that most men weren't.

Reno gently brushed his knuckles against her cheek. "We need to head home before the next band of snow showers moves through. Don't worry about the kids, princess. They don't need a bunch of shit. We didn't raise them to think that way."

"I know. It's just that… I grew up doing without, and…"

April's doleful eyes looked down at her empty basket, the cheap bottles rolling around and clacking against each other. It was a heck of a lot more than what she'd ever gotten for Christmas in the years following her father's death. Maybe coming from nothing was what compelled her to give more, now that she had a good job and a nice home. Lexi was gifting

Mel a special necklace that she'd had since she was a teen, and Naya's gift was going to be a mentorship with one of her associates who worked in fashion. April wanted her present to mean something special, and what she'd picked out was embarrassingly inadequate.

Reno wrapped his arms around her and lifted her off her feet. He pressed a chaste kiss to her mouth and began walking. "I don't like that look. My girl isn't going to be sad on Christmas. I ain't gonna sugarcoat it for you. If Mel doesn't like that damn polish, we're going to have words."

April laughed against his thick neck as he weaved around a couple in the greeting card aisle. "I know you're right, but it's my fault for waiting—"

Reno cleared his throat. "Finish that sentence and I'm tossing you in the snow."

She lifted her head and met his gaze. "Don't even *think* about it, or we won't be spooning for a week."

He paused in front of the wrapping paper and smirked with those thin lips of his. "Yes, ma'am."

Two women were gawking at them, undoubtedly wondering what a tough guy like Reno was doing holding a woman who thought fashion was oversized sweatpants tucked inside her brown Uggs.

She cupped his face in her hands and kissed him passionately, giving extra attention to the tiny scar on his lip. Despite the scented lotion on his neck, his musky cologne—right along with the light stubble on his face—was driving her wild. Her sudden public display of affection caught him off guard, and he took a step back, knocking over bags of tissue paper and ribbons.

"You can put me down now," she whispered.

"Hot damn." He set her down and pulled a box of candy off the shelf. "Kids like chocolate."

Reno put his arm around her, and they went to the register to pay for the items. She swooned. No matter how many years passed, Reno always had a way of making her feel like they were a young couple in love.

As soon as they opened the door to leave, a gust of wind blew an army of snowflakes at them. April hurried to the Challenger, Reno right behind her. He opened her door and helped her in before crossing around to his side.

April shivered, still in disbelief that they were having such an unexpected white winter. She couldn't remember the last time they had snow, let alone this much. They were comparing it to a snowstorm in the 1930s, so she had to laugh when she looked inside the store and saw a man walking around in a pair of long shorts and a light jacket.

Reno hopped in and slammed the door. "Damn, it's nippy out there."

"Not as nippy as it would have been on your bike."

He put his hand on her upper thigh and gave it a light

squeeze. "Your idea to take a car was better. It's cozy in here. Roomy. And we're not due back for another hour."

"Is that so?" She smiled and averted her gaze out the window.

April was too old to be coy. Even though she'd stopped aging just shy of forty, a part of her would always feel like the young girl who fell in love with Reno all those years ago. The one who knew exactly what she wanted and yet was uncertain how to navigate through life's difficult decisions.

Her breath fogged the window, and she drew a little heart.

"Is that a yes?" he asked, his voice smoky.

"Isn't there some kind of sacred rule about having sex in your brother's car?"

Reno squeezed her knee and slid his gaze down to her lips as she licked them. "Nope."

April quickly realized this friendly game of flirtation was treading dangerous ground. "Reno, we can't just hijack Austin's car. And besides, there's no room back there," she said, turning to look in the backseat.

Her eyes widened.

Reno patted his seat. "Who says we have to get in the back? Let's see how far this seat reclines. What's wrong?"

How can this be? April looked around in disbelief. Reno had locked the doors before they went inside; she'd seen it with her own eyes.

"Reno, when did you buy that?"

"Buy what?" He shifted to see what held April's attention. "What the fuck?"

Reno reached in the backseat and retrieved a leather quiver with a shiny red ribbon wrapped around it. Inside was a modest set of arrows fletched with feathers. "This bag is handmade."

"I didn't put it there."

"Me neither."

"Do you think Austin or Lexi stashed gifts in the car?"

He scanned their surroundings. "I cleaned it out before we left. It sure as hell wasn't back there when we got here, and I locked both doors when we headed inside."

April took the quiver and studied the craftsmanship. When something on the strap caught her eye, she tilted it to get a better look. Burned into the leather was one word: Melody.

A shiver ran down her spine.

This was exactly what Mel needed—a gift she would love. The quiver she used now was falling apart. Melody liked target practice, a skill acquired from her grandmother. Archery was a source of strength and accomplishment, and Melody was a natural.

"Is there something you're not telling me?" Reno asked.

In disbelief, April regarded him for a moment and cracked a smile. "Yeah. I think I just met Santa Claus in the deodorant aisle."

CHAPTER 3

Trevor and William

"I't's noon, and we're still in bed," Trevor grumbled. His complaint belied the satisfaction in his tone and reluctance to move, but he felt like he had to say something about their vegetative state.

William snuggled behind him and murmured against his neck. "I can't think of any other place I'd rather be than right here, right now, with you."

"Maybe we should make ourselves useful and shovel snow. They say we're going to get eight more inches."

Trevor sucked in a sharp breath when William's hand roamed south.

"Indeed."

It was Christmas Eve, and the holiday season had become a thing of tradition in the Weston pack. Maybe not normal tradition as depicted on television, but the pack spent their holiday playing pool, working puzzles, drinking, eating good food, and listening to the kids botch Christmas carols with their alternative versions. So Trevor felt a little shitty staying isolated in the bedroom.

Last night, Trevor and William retired early and stayed up half the night talking. Early that morning, they stayed in bed doing other things.

William had landed in Trevor's life like a gift, and sometimes it seemed too good to be true. Trevor had never felt more connected to anyone. He grew up believing he was undeserving of not only love but also a pack. He had endured years of torment and abuse—verbal and physical—from his own packmates, who'd singled him out as different. Men who were supposed to honor brotherhood and protect their own. They made him ashamed of being a Shifter. After he split from the pack, the abuse continued in subsequent relationships. April had taught him to love his wolf, but it was William who taught Trevor to love himself.

William was the first man who had never berated or hit him, and it took Trevor time to get used to it. After all, he'd spent most of his life in the closet and always kept his relationships secret, so it was thrilling and equally terrifying when William would put his arm around him in public.

For the past two hours, they'd been lying in bed, listening to their pack bustling in the outside hall, occasionally knocking their fists against Trevor's door in an effort to summon them out of bed.

Well, Trevor and William's door.

After the mating ceremony, William moved out of his tiny downstairs room. Best of all, Trevor didn't have to throw out his model airplanes to make room for his mate. Maybe a few extra drawers were full, but William didn't even want to upgrade the bed from a full to a queen. He said he liked keeping it simple and even joked about downsizing to a twin.

Of the two, William was the protector. Sometimes he'd shift into his wolf and lie at the foot of the bed to guard Trevor, as if danger lurked in the wee hours of the night. William had witnessed a lot of tragedy in his time, and maybe that had something to do with him becoming the dominant one in the relationship. Trevor didn't mind. He loved the feeling of having a protector—someone who would look out for him and always stand by his side. He'd never experienced that kind of unconditional devotion from a lover before.

Trevor turned around to face his mate. William's messy curls were unruly and sexy—just like that short beard he was attempting to grow. Trevor pinched at it. "Are you going to keep this?"

"Perhaps. My face gets cold in the winter."

Trevor nipped William's stubbly chin. "As long as I can find your lips in there, I'm okay with it."

William had a way of smiling with his brown eyes. They were large and expressive, and his gaze could stare right into a man's soul. "Mustn't get so attached to physical attributes. I'd still love you if you had a thick bed of chest hair or shaved your head."

"Good, 'cause I was thinking about getting grills for my teeth." He smiled wide. "What do you think? Gold or diamonds?"

William propped his head in his hand. "If you cap your teeth, I'll still love you. We'll just have to live in seclusion like two hermits. They'll whisper about us at peace parties, and your gold teeth will become a cautionary tale for young children."

Trevor shifted his naked body closer to William and kissed his Adam's apple. "Ah, so you *do* care what other people think."

"If that were true, I wouldn't have proposed in a public place."

"A bowling alley," Trevor reminded him. "And the pack had no idea you were even gay."

William drew in his bottom lip and wet it. "I concealed my sexuality to maintain stability within the pack, but you lived in the closet out of fear. Even now when we go out in public, you're afraid to take my hand."

Trevor rolled onto his back. William didn't understand. He'd never endured the kind of ridicule and torment that Trevor had, and that kind of pain sank into your marrow and became a part of you. Public opinion meant little to him; it was the fear of being targeted. Now he had something to lose. "You were Lorenzo's second-in-command, Will. We all know what a douche he can be. Are you telling me there wasn't a sliver of fear behind your decision to stay quiet about it?"

William pinched his chin. "Not the same type of fear you've dealt with in the past. The beta is the glue that holds the pack together. If the pack can't respect the second-in-command, then they won't respect the Packmaster. I didn't hide who I was in fear of persecution or even retaliation; I wanted to keep the peace. My motives were driven by the pack's needs. But all that's changed now."

Trevor turned back on his side and focused on a tiny freckle on William's left cheek. "You ever think about changing packs to promote yourself back to second?"

William tucked his arm beneath the pillow. "In the beginning I did. But what more could I want that I don't have now? I'm not an egomaniac, and as the third in rank, I back Reno's decisions. The pack respects me, and I've come to realize over the years what's important."

"And what's that?"

William traced his finger down Trevor's cheek. "Family. I didn't have that connection with Enzo's pack. You have to decide which sacrifices are worth making to live a fulfilled life. Wouldn't you agree?"

The night-light went out, as did the sound of the heater. Their room was located in the center of the house where there weren't any windows, so they were drenched in darkness.

Trevor pushed himself halfway up. "Was that the power?"

The sound of feet tramping down the stairs came from the end of the hall—probably the twins, who were on the brink of becoming young men. The two of them were a cohesive pair who respected each other and were eager to contribute to the pack. They helped Reno chop and stack wood, learned basic home repairs, and occasionally sat with Austin when he was discussing general Packmaster issues with the Council or other local Packmasters. Since the boys were alphas, Austin was grooming them for a future as strong leaders.

William crawled over Trevor and accidentally elbowed him in the eye. "Apologies."

"No biggie. Just my eyeball."

William stumbled and fell on the floor. "Do you remember where I put my trousers?"

"What happened?" Izzy yelled from the hallway.

"The power's out," Ben replied. "Austin's calling up the electric company to see what's going on."

"Hell's bells."

Trevor found a pair of sweats on the floor and yanked them on just seconds before the door opened. Flashlight beams twirled around in the darkness as he stepped into the hall.

"Where's Reno?" Izzy asked.

Ben aimed the light at her face. "He went out with April. Looks like Will's the man in charge."

William must have heard his name. He appeared in the doorway, fully dressed in a loose pair of jeans and Trevor's button-up shirt, which was a little too tight on him. "Close off the outside rooms. We need to keep the heat centralized. If ice took down the power lines, then this could last a lot longer than a few hours. Someone needs to seal off the windows downstairs with blankets."

Ben handed Trevor a spare flashlight. "I'm on it." Without delay, he rushed down the hall.

Trevor scratched his unshaven jaw. "What do you want me to do?"

William devised a plan of action on the spot. His expertise with managing a pack was undeniable. "Go stoke the fire. The last thing we need is a dying fire and an open flue. Make sure Ben closes the drapes in the unused rooms. Oh, and put towels beneath those doors. I don't know that it'll help much, but every little bit matters."

Izzy reached in her pocket for a small band and tied up her red hair. "I'll bring all the blankets downstairs." She covered her mouth. "Oh no!"

Trevor stepped forward, his adrenaline kicking into gear. "What's wrong?"

"The food. Lynn's been in the kitchen all morning, chopping up vegetables and preparing everything for dinner. She was going to put the turkey in the oven around one."

William sighed. "We can't worry about that right now. Do we have any more flashlights?"

Trevor thought about it. "Austin has a drawer in his office

with a bunch of emergency supplies, and there's probably some in the garage. I'll check inside the vehicles and see if I can find anything useful."

"Good. We need to gather up all the light sources we can find, including candles."

Jericho strode out of the bathroom just as cool as a cucumber. "What's shakin' out here? I had to piss in the dark."

Izzy shined the flashlight onto his ripped-up jeans. "The power's out. You might want to put on something warmer, honey bunny."

His eyes skimmed down her long legs. Izzy had on a pair of sleep shorts and green slippers. "Then I volunteer to wear *you*, Sexybelle."

She jutted her hip and flashed him an annoyed look.

"Reno's still gone," William informed him. "I want you to run outside into the garage and bring in all the flashlights and lanterns you can find. It'll be dark in a few hours, and if the power doesn't come back on, we don't need to be wandering around in the dark in search of things. A dark house is an open invitation for rogues, so let's put a few of those lanterns on the front porch."

The idea of rogues left Trevor unsettled. He always thought of electricity as an invisible thread that connected people to civilized behavior. Without it, humans looted and turned to violence. Shifters, on the other hand, plotted attacks and stole land.

Jericho shook back his long hair and winked as he swaggered by. "Gotcha."

Izzy snapped her fingers and ran down the hall. "Blankets."

As they headed downstairs, Trevor considered the idea of sealing off the staircase with a hanging blanket. Maybe that would keep some of the heat from escaping the first floor. He also did a mental check of where all the candles in the house were located, but Lynn would know for certain. The men knew better than to touch her candles after the time Reno had boxed them up and stored them in the garage.

During a heat wave.

Once downstairs, they stepped around Ben, who was cutting a large piece of foam. "I found some insulation in the storage room," he announced.

Trevor grimaced. "I think that's Jericho's soundproofing equipment."

Ben stood up and blanched. He was Wheeler's identical twin, but the two couldn't be more opposite. Sometimes they finished each other's sentences, but their mannerisms and style were uniquely their own. Since rejoining the pack, Ben was a changed man from the old version Trevor remembered. He was more aware of how his actions affected the pack, and not just because he didn't want to get kicked out again. Ben had found redemption, and everyone could see the light in his eyes when he was around his brothers.

Ben stared down at the foam with a look of regret. "He's gonna kill me in my sleep."

William patted his shoulder. "Mustn't worry over trivial matters. I'm sure Jericho wouldn't value his personal belongings over his family's safety. If he says anything to you about it, tell him it was on my order. Foam can be replaced."

Lennon and Hendrix raced into the room. "Uncle Reno's gone," Hendrix declared, out of breath. "What do you want us to do?"

Hendrix had on a red shirt and Lennon blue. It made Trevor want to put on a pair of 3-D glasses.

Will pinched his chin and studied the boys. "Why don't you two bring in a stack of firewood and pile it in the kitchen by the washer. Let's keep the wood dry, and make sure the tarp is secure when you're done."

They both saluted him before scrambling toward the kitchen.

"Keep the door closed!" William shouted.

Trevor barked out a laugh. "With that kind of enthusiasm, maybe you should have told them to shovel the driveway."

William winked at him. "No, I'm saving that one for Denver."

"You better pick someone else," Maizy informed him. They hadn't noticed her curled up on the sofa. "Denny went out with Wheeler to find a tree."

Lexi entered the room and folded her arms. "Well, it's

official. We have no power. Austin called Prince, and he confirmed that several power lines are down. The electric company is putting everyone on hold, and no one can get any information on how long we'll have to wait."

Trevor twirled his flashlight. "On a good note, this is Texas, so it'll probably be eighty degrees by the weekend."

Lexi stood on the hearth. "Okay, Mr. Funnyman. If the power doesn't come back on by then, *you'll* be the ones outside scrubbing laundry on a washboard."

"Is Austin in his office?" William rounded the couch. "I'll let him know I'm mobilizing the pack into action. If anyone finds themselves with nothing to do, tell them to wait in here for my orders."

Izzy jogged down the stairs with an armload of blankets. She set them against the staircase wall and took a breather.

Trevor crossed the room and placed another log on the grate, but he couldn't stop thinking about his best girl and Reno being out in this mess. He'd always felt like a watchdog to April. They were inseparable, and even though she now looked physically older than him, April was the little sister he never had.

He kept his eyes on the bright flames. "Has April called?"

The second Izzy's phone rang, she darted across the room and snatched it off the TV stand. "This is the party to whom you are speaking." After a beat, she snapped her fingers at Trevor. "They're on their way back. It's taking them longer because of the roads. The overpasses are starting to freeze." Then she turned away. "Yeah, I'm here. Trevor was asking about you. … Okay, you two. Be careful."

Trevor closed the screen on the hearth and stood up. "Maybe I should go after them. They might need help if something goes wrong."

"Maybe you need to stay right here," Maizy said, tossing her lap blanket aside. "Reno's looking after her, so you've got nothing to worry about. That's one man I'd want by my side in a postapocalyptic world, and don't tell Denver I said that."

"What if their car breaks down?"

"Then he'll build one out of sticks. The only thing we should be concerned about is whether or not Reno will bring Austin's car back in one piece."

Lexi chuckled. "Don't even say it out loud. Austin loves that car."

Still lying on her back, Maizy crossed her legs dramatically. "Not as much as you do."

Lexi blushed and looked as if she wanted to hit her little sister with a pillow.

This is going to be a long day, Trevor thought. He glanced down at his bare chest, and it was then that he realized his sweatpants were on backward.

The girls noticed it too and waggled their brows at him.

"Sparty! Baby, where are you?" Naya called out.

"Probably sleeping in the dryer again," Lexi suggested.

Naya's tight red shirt had one of those keyhole openings in the front, and everyone could see her cleavage. She was the one person in the pack who didn't look like an anemic Irishman in winter. Her brown skin glowed as if she'd just returned from a cruise in the Caribbean. Naya stopped behind the couch and pursed her ruby-red lips. "He always hides when it's chilly outside. I just want to make sure he doesn't get locked up in one of these rooms or in a closet."

Trevor scratched his neck. "That cat has mad survival skills. Let him sleep. There's going to be a lot of us going in and out for the next few hours, so better that he's out of the way. I think we all need to put on warmer clothes. Will's handing out assignments."

Lexi's shoulders sagged. "My mom's in the kitchen, panicking over dinner. Maddox is trying to help, but you know how that goes. It won't all fit in the fridge. She cooked some things ahead of time to reheat later, and now she thinks Christmas is ruined."

Maizy swung her legs off the sofa and stood up. "I'll help. All we need to do is fill the coolers with some ice or snow and put them out back. No meat though, or it'll attract wild animals."

"I have such a smart sister," Lexi gushed. "Let me see if I can give Maddox something to do. He doesn't seem to realize that women need to be left alone when they're in crisis mode."

"Darling, I never panic," Naya purred. "And you're

forgetting the fridge in the heat house. It'll stay cold for a few more hours."

Lexi snapped her fingers and hurried out of the room.

"Spartacus!" Naya sang.

Trevor chuckled. If there was one thing Naya panicked over, it was her pet cat. Sparty was an independent fellow, and Naya would work herself into a frenzy if he went missing for more than a few hours. Trevor could only imagine what would happen if she ever had kids.

Melody burst through the front door, snow clinging to her striped hat. "What's going on? Dad's outside digging around in the garage. Why are all the curtains closed?"

"Power outage," Trevor said. "Nothing to worry about."

Melody raised a quizzical brow. "We're buried in snow, and he says it's nothing to worry about."

Melody was blossoming into a beautiful young woman at seventeen. She marched to the beat of her own drum, and part of that probably had to do with her parents. She was always dyeing her hair different colors, and this year she'd chosen violet with silver streaks. The edgy cut fell slightly past her shoulders and looked like she hadn't brushed it since yesterday.

Naya clicked her tongue several times and scanned the room.

"Is Sparty missing in action again?" Mel asked. "I'll help you look for him."

"Would you, darling? I'll check upstairs if you search down here."

Mel twirled out of her coat and hung it up. "I know all his favorite hiding spots."

The two dispersed to begin the hunt.

Trevor admired the wreath over the fireplace. Someone had strewn tiny multicolored lights around the living room, but it seemed depressingly dark without them on. He took a seat on the hearth, feeling useless. They'd never had a snowstorm like this, and he didn't know what the hell to do. Stuffing a few towels beneath the doors hardly seemed like an important job.

"Is something troubling you?" William cut between the furniture and hovered over him.

It was the notion Trevor would always have in the back of his mind—no matter how irrational—of not belonging. It was a bullshit feeling, especially with all the love in this pack. But people who haven't survived trauma will never understand the battle scars that remain. For years afterward, he fell into a pattern of abusive relationships. Trevor wasn't a father with kids to look after, or a second-in-command delegating tasks, nor was he a relation to anyone in the pack by blood. He worked in a bakery and sometimes sang a few tunes for extra cash—not exactly the go-to guy when there was trouble. Of all of them, he was probably the most expendable.

Just once, he wanted to be the hero.

William knelt and rested his forearms on his knees. "Don't

think I'm not familiar with that look. Everyone here respects you whether you realize it or not. You're a shining example of bravery to them because of your struggles. What are your thoughts on what else needs to be done? I feel like I've covered everything, but I'm not certain."

Trevor rubbed the sleep out of his eyes. "Extra batteries. The flashlights will run out, and this could last for days. If the power's still out tomorrow, everyone can take turns charging their phones in one of the cars. We're all here, so it's not a big deal. But someone from the outside may need to get ahold of us. All this shit needs to be unplugged in case we get a power surge when it comes back on."

"Good thinking." William's gaze drifted to the fireplace. "I'll have Maddox take care of unplugging the electronics and switching off the lights. It'll give him something productive to do. Did you watch the weather report this week to see how long this would last?"

"Two more days of steady snow," Trevor replied. "Today, Christmas Day, and the day after. Then it's clouds, but the temperature isn't going up until after the weekend."

William rose to his feet, hands on his hips. "I wonder if we need to shovel the driveway again."

"It won't matter. We can clear the private road all we want, but the city never sands down the main road. We're off their radar. Shovel to your heart's content, but it's a waste of time if we can't get out on the city roads."

William locked his fingers behind his head and turned. It gave Trevor a chance to admire his svelte body—especially since Trevor's shirt was a size too small and rising up. Tight muscles in all the right places, his jeans hanging low and revealing the V-cut in his abdomen. Trevor had always been attracted to William, who was older, more mature, and not interested. Or so Trevor had thought. He'd never met anyone who was better than him at hiding his sexuality, and William was so casual about coming out that it made Trevor wish he had that same level of confidence. Trevor's eyes slid down and noticed the button on William's jeans was undone.

"Something on your mind?" William asked, his voice so sexy that it rolled across Trevor's skin and gave him goose bumps.

Trevor stood up and wrapped his arms around him. "I thought of a better way to keep warm."

"And what's that?"

"Body heat."

"Indeed." William reciprocated, holding him close. "There was something important I forgot to tell you this morning."

"What's that?"

He pressed his scruffy cheek against Trevor's. "I love you."

CHAPTER 4

Wheeler and Denver

WHEELER CRESTED A SHORT HILL and stared at row upon row of Christmas trees. Fir, pine, and another variety he couldn't identify. A blanket of snow rolled out before him, and the trees were iced in the white stuff like one of Lexi's cupcakes. Denver was being a picky bastard and bypassing anything that didn't meet his standards. Either it was too big, too small, too wide, or too scrawny.

Goldi-fucking-locks had nothing on this kid.

They must have been out there for two hours—long enough that Denver told him all about their irrigation system and the importance of supporting farmers.

Fat flakes of snow drifted in front of him, and he trudged forward, trying to keep his boots in line with Denver's footprints so that more snow wouldn't seep its way into the crevices. He had an axe in one hand and the keys to the truck in the other.

"Go pick out a tree, they said. It'll be *fun*, they said." He swung the axe and struck a nearby branch. Had he known Denver would take his sweet-ass time picking out the perfect tree, he might have dressed in something warmer than a leather bomber jacket. The sheepskin lining and collar helped, but what he needed was a damn hat. Even his circle beard was collecting snow. Gloves would have been nice, but *no*. Denver had promised it would be an in-and-out operation.

Wheeler should have known better. Denver didn't even approach sex as an in-and-out operation. It was more like an all-day invasion.

Wind battered Wheeler's face, flecks of ice getting in his eyes. "Come on, Puffy! Get your ass moving and pick out a tree before they call out a search party for us."

He quickened his pace and decided the first tree he saw Denver standing next to was coming down. They'd already paid the guy in advance.

Denver was barely visible in that ridiculous white coat. When he turned around, his grin was so wide that it put a rosy hue on his cheeks. "I found the perfect one."

"Move aside, Puffy."

Wheeler kicked aside the snow until he saw a patch of dead grass. The branches were low to the ground, so he had to kneel to reach the trunk.

"Think it'll fit in the truck?" Denver asked conversationally.

The axe struck the wood, and a few chips broke away. "We'll make it fit if I have to cut it in half."

"What's up your ass?"

Wheeler glared up through an opening in the branches. "Oh, I don't know. About seven inches of snow?"

"Should have worn a coat like mine," he said, tucking his hands in the pockets.

"Back up before I accidentally shred that jacket apart with my blade. 'Preciate ya."

Denver circled to the other side of the tree and shook the limbs. A large chunk of snow fell on Wheeler's neck and slid down the back of his jacket.

"So what did you get Naya?" Denver asked.

Wheeler's blade struck the wood and wedged in so tight he had to wiggle the axe free. "Lingerie."

Denver coughed and laughed at the same time. "That's not a gift for her; that's a gift for *you*."

"My gift comes later."

When Denver shook the tree again, Wheeler sat back and stared daggers at him.

Denver rubbed his red nose. "I got Maizy a new laptop."

"What was wrong with the old one?"

"Nothing."

"So now she has to transfer all her shit over to a new one?"

Denver regarded him for a moment, and Wheeler could sense panic. "Are you goading me? She needs a spare in case something happens to that one. She does all her work on the computer, dickwad."

Wheeler shook his head and continued chopping the tree, now wondering if he'd screwed up his own gift exchange. Naya always managed to outdo him. He'd thought tattooing a panther on his chest for their mating ceremony would get him off the hook for life. What the hell more could a woman want? Now he had to contend with holidays and anniversaries.

Wheeler just wasn't that creative.

Denver heaved a sigh. "Why didn't you bring the bow saw instead? An axe is a little old-fashioned."

"So is cutting down a damn tree in the woods when they sell them on street corners. Your point?"

One final swing and Wheeler pushed the tree over.

Denver howled with excitement. "How much do you think it weighs?"

Wheeler stood up, out of breath. "I guess you'll find out when you drag it back to the truck."

"I'm not doing this by myself."

Wheeler wiped the snow out of his hair. "What's the matter, sweetheart? Afraid of doing man's work?"

Denver's hood covered his entire head, and the only thing visible was his face. "I drove. I picked it out. I paid for it out of my own pocket. Since you volunteered to come, you need to volunteer to help."

"I cut down the damn tree."

"Does that make you a big boy?"

Wheeler threw his axe in the snow. "And boom goes the

dynamite." He shifted, and Denver stumbled backward before taking off, chunks of snow flying from beneath his shoes. Wheeler's wolf was tangled up in his damn jeans, so Denver got a good head start. Once free, Wheeler bounded through the snow, giving chase.

"Cut it out, Wheeler!" Denver yelled, weaving around the trees.

Wheeler was still aware and decided not to let his wolf take complete control, but he might as well give Denver a good workout. He nipped the back of Denver's jacket, and it made a ripping sound.

"Hey! That's my new jacket, you mutt!"

Mutt?

This time Wheeler's wolf bit Denver's ass. He fell flat on his face, arms and legs spread wide.

Satisfied, Wheeler shifted back. Maybe it wasn't the most well-thought-out plan. His clothes were a good hike away, and it was damn nippy.

Denver rolled over, his face covered with a light dusting of the powdery stuff. "I hate you."

"Yeah, yeah. You've been saying that since you were three." A heavy wall of snowflakes pelted them. "We need to get the hell out of here."

Denver waved his arms and legs in a rhythmic motion. When he finished, he stood up and stared down at his snow angel. "Maybe we should move to Colorado. I like snow."

"You also like Doritos. Does that mean we should move to the chip factory?"

Denver scooped a handful of snow off his head and, with a relaxed smile, smashed it against Wheeler's bare chest.

Wheeler didn't have time for this shit. They'd already wasted enough hours in the day, and the second storm was moving in soon. That meant at least another five inches from what the weathermen were saying, but they liked to disagree a lot in order to get people to watch their channel. He stalked toward the fallen tree, the soles of his feet freezing.

Not nearly as much as his balls.

Denver sneezed and ran past him.

The one thing Wheeler appreciated about the men in his pack being mostly related was that they never took shit personally. A lot of wolf packs were comprised of unrelated people, and while the bond and brotherhood was there, it seemed like there was more opportunity for friction within the house. It was good to horse around with his brothers and not have it escalate. Denver could have shifted into his crazy-ass wolf, but that might have spawned a real fight with blood and hurt feelings.

The only person who'd ever crossed the line was Ben, and it had taken a long time for his brother to get his shit together. Sometimes being without family puts things in perspective for a man. It was damn good to have him back, and since all their secrets were out, the tension that used to exist between them was gone. Wheeler loved his twin; he'd die for him. Always felt that way and always would.

When he neared the fallen tree, he caught sight of Denver hurling his pants as far as he could. They landed on top of a tall tree a few rows over.

Wheeler ignored him and put on his socks and underwear.

"Give me the keys and I'll warm up the truck," Denver said.

After Wheeler put on his shoes, he hoisted the tree by the trunk.

"Where the hell are the keys?"

Wheeler lifted his leather jacket with one finger and gave him a sardonic smile. "In the pocket of my jeans. Go fetch."

CHAPTER 5

Kat and Prince

KAT HOLLERED WITH DELIGHT WHEN her skis skated to the left and she almost fell. That might have given her seven-hundred-year-old boyfriend a coronary. She gripped the rope that was tethered to the large silver truck in front of her. Not Prince's truck, but one of his packmates had lent it to them.

Prince glared at her through the back window, and she waved blithely at him.

When not doing investigative work, Kat was a homebody. Her job was exhausting, and lying on the sofa to get her sitcom fix was the one thing she looked forward to. Well, aside from Prince giving her a bath. But all bets were off when it came to crazy outdoor recreation elicited by a good old-fashioned snowstorm. This was nothing compared to what she'd seen up north, but enough of it was packed on the roads to make it worth venturing out.

Naturally, seeing her fishtail from the back of the pickup

truck was eating Prince alive, but he never forbade her from doing what she wanted. Prince wasn't her father, nor was he her Packmaster. Besides, women like her couldn't be tamed of their adventurous ways. She understood his desire to protect her from danger; it was the one quality she loved most about him.

Kat had spent the past two nights at his mansion enjoying the scenic view of snowfall in the country. But staying inside became torture, especially after finding a pair of skis hidden in a storage room. The initial plan had been to find a hill where she could test them out, but Prince didn't know of a suitable slope that was clear of trees. Aside from that, climbing back up the hill sucked the fun out of that idea. When she noticed rope in the back of the truck, she hatched her plan.

Kat sneezed. She couldn't feel her nose anymore and probably looked like Rudolph being dragged down the road by a half-ton truck. It hadn't occurred to her to bring a ski mask, but the goggles protected her eyes, and the red-and-white hat kept her hair dry.

Only two cars had passed, one of the drivers giving her a "you're an idiot" stare and the other recording it on his phone. Sanding trucks didn't come out this far, and without traffic, country roads were ideal for this kind of tomfoolery.

The truck slowed to a stop, white smoke billowing from the exhaust.

Kat dropped the rope and bent over to catch her breath.

She mentally kicked herself for not having brought drinks and food; nothing sounded better to quench her thirst than root beer.

And nothing went better with root beer than hamburgers and onion rings.

Her stomach growled.

Prince got out of the truck, his black boots crunching on the snow as he swaggered toward her, looking all dapper in his long wool coat and black hat. "Have you had enough of this foolishness?"

She snickered. "That depends. Is the lake frozen over?"

"Very amusing." He removed her goggles, and his brows gathered in a frown. "You need to get warm."

"What did you have in mind?"

"Removing your boots and sitting in front of the heater."

"My tummy's all aflutter." Kat fell against his broad chest. "If you want to keep me warm, then snuggle with me, Charming." She wrapped her arms inside his coat and nuzzled her cold face in the crook of his neck. "You smell yummy."

"This is the most inane thing I've ever done. If my packmates saw what you were doing—"

"They would have cheered along," she finished. "Russell would have sat in the back and swung the rope around, taking bets on how long I could hold on."

Prince lowered his head. "And that's why he stayed behind."

She kissed his smooth chin. "I would have taken that bet."

"Why must you behave so foolishly? You could have injured yourself."

She sneezed and backed away to rub her nose. "I track dangerous men for a living. I've been shot, stabbed, and I jumped off a bridge. Do you think a little ski ride is really that dangerous in the grand scheme of things?"

His eyes, one sapphire and one brown, sparkled like gemstones. "Sometimes I think you do these things to get a rise out of me and not because you want to do them."

Kat smiled sheepishly because it was partly true. She was more carefree than Prince, and she liked ruffling his ancient feathers. Nothing was sexier than when the testosterone floodgates burst open and he was willing to do anything to protect his woman. Her alpha wolf responded to that kind of chivalrous behavior, and maybe that was why she hadn't changed her risky lifestyle.

"Do you want to go next?" she asked.

His jaw clenched, and she burst out laughing. Kat gathered up the rope and began singing "Let It Snow," putting emphasis on the part about the fire being so delightful.

Once they got back to his place, her plan was to light a fire in his bedroom and make s'mores. Whether he liked them or not was irrelevant. The idea of Prince stretched out shirtless in front of a fire, licking chocolate, was enough to make her toes curl in her snow boots. She tossed the rope into the back of the truck along with the goggles.

"Watch out," he said. "Someone's coming."

She peered around the side of the truck and squinted. Another vehicle headed toward them, and just as it crossed over a small bridge, the tires lost traction, and it skidded off the road.

Prince jogged ahead while she detached the skis from her boots and then followed after him.

"Is that one of the Cole brothers?" she yelled out, recognizing the blue truck. She didn't know the Weston pack very well, but she'd worked closely with Reno and had met them once at a peace party after the war. Prince spoke highly of their Packmaster, but that wasn't the sole reason for him running to their aid. Prince was the kind of man who would render assistance to anyone in distress—even Girl Scouts trying to sell enough cookies to meet quota.

The truck stopped at a precarious angle down in the ditch. Two men got out, one of them wearing the most ridiculous white coat, and the other—Well, the other one was Wheeler. He didn't have on a shirt, just a whole lot of tattoos, which made him easy to identify.

"Do you need some help?" Prince offered.

Wheeler folded his arms and glanced back at his packmate, who fell facedown into the snow. "I need another minute to decide."

Kat waved. "Hey."

Wheeler nodded a hello.

The man in the puffy white coat stood up and scowled at Wheeler. "Next time I say hold the wheel, do me a favor: hold the wheel."

Kat recognized Denver by his blue eyes and wavy blond hair. He looked sweaty, and by the looks of his broken zipper, he must have been trying to remove his coat while driving.

Denver kicked the tire. "Our ass is grass if we don't get this tree home."

Wheeler calmly looked skyward, a storm brewing in his eyes. Kat wondered why he was only half-dressed, but she had a feeling it explained his hair-trigger mood.

"Let's give them a ride home," Kat suggested. "The tree will fit in the bed of the truck."

"Let's see if it'll fit up your ass," Wheeler grumbled at Denver.

His brother strode past him. "Shut it." He stood beside Prince and sized up his truck. "Do you have a chain in the back to pull us out? We can't leave our wheels in the ditch."

"No, but I have a rope."

Kat chuckled. "That'll snap like a woman getting a gym membership from her boyfriend on Valentine's Day. What you need is a chain."

Prince gave her a sideways glance, but she saw humor twinkling in those eyes. He didn't always get her jokes, but when he did, it was pure magic. Rarely did she rouse laughter out of him. Most ancients were impassive, so that's why Kat appreciated those little moments.

Denver stuffed his hands into his coat pockets. "It might work if someone pushes the truck from the front."

Wheeler kicked snow at him. "And that someone is you, sweetheart."

"Contrary to what my woman says, I'm not Hercules. And if that rope snaps, I'm roadkill."

"So what are you trying to say, brother? That my life is worth less?"

Denver shrugged. "I do dishes and drive the tractor mower in the summer. That makes me a keeper."

Kat offered up a suggestion before they started a brawl. "Say, why don't both of you push while I steer it in reverse? Two is always better than one." She took off her gloves and stuffed them into her coat pockets while waiting for an answer. These two were like an Abbott and Costello act.

After Prince headed back to his truck, Wheeler retrieved a leather jacket from inside their vehicle and put it on. Kat stepped aside while Prince backed up until Denver knocked on the tailgate to signal him to stop. From there, they tied the other end of the rope to the hitch.

Once secure, they shared a moment of silence as they looked between the two vehicles.

"How heavy is that tree?" Kat asked. "Maybe you should take it out and lighten the load."

Denver held his arms out wide when Wheeler motioned to get it. "Skedaddle. Let the pro take care of this."

Wheeler folded his arms. "Mayhap the pro is going to need a little help."

"Fine. But if you break one limb off this tree, we're turning around and picking out a new one."

"Works for me. But only one of us is coming back."

Kat realized the two of them must have gone through hell to get that tree.

Packmates often rile each other up. The ones who don't get along learn to walk away before a fight breaks out. Arguing is the wolf's natural way of asserting dominance, even when ranks are established. She guessed the dynamic of true brotherhood was a little different. People who share the same blood are often more tolerant of each other. That was something Kat knew all about. She and her sister bickered, but it wasn't enough to erode the loyalty she felt.

Denver and Wheeler set the tree down on some fresh snow that wasn't muddied from tires, then circled to the front of the vehicle and waited. Kat slid down the slope and almost fell before regaining her footing. The driver's side door was hanging open, so she climbed in.

The heavy smell of beef jerky made her mouth water. She spied the bag in the passenger seat and wedged a piece into her mouth when the men weren't looking. The moment they swung their eyes up, she stopped chewing and smiled.

Kat fired up the engine, and when the back end of the truck jerked, Wheeler shouted, "Now!"

She reversed gears and hit the gas. The two brothers shoved the front end, a grimace on their red faces. The truck lurched, but Kat couldn't get any traction beneath the tires as the engine hummed loudly.

Denver yelled at Prince, waving his arm. "Hold up!"

Kat put the brakes on and watched him hike up the incline until he moved out of sight.

Wheeler rested his forearms on the hood, and when he put his head down, Kat shoved another piece of jerky into her mouth. All that skiing had worked up her appetite, and if they didn't get this show on the road, her ravenous wolf was going to come out and go hunting. Too bad all the good Mexican restaurants were closed. Tacos sounded perfect right about now.

And queso.

Wheeler looked up when Denver returned. "What the hell were you busy doing?"

"Putting something down for traction."

Kat waited for Prince to get back in his truck, and when his brake lights flashed, she dropped her foot on the gas.

The engine whined, and the moment the truck lurched, she put more weight on the pedal. Denver and Wheeler's faces were bright red as they shoved the front end of the truck. It occurred to her that if the rope snapped, the truck could slide right over them.

"Push harder!" she yelled.

They scowled at her the way a woman in labor might if given the same orders.

Kat howled with victory when the tire went over a bump and they were back on the road.

"Stop!" Denver bellowed, his eyes wide.

She hit the brake, her heart pounding. An irrational thought flew through her head that the bump she'd hit was Prince.

Denver ran around to the back and dragged the Christmas tree out of the way.

Wheeler approached the driver's side and leaned on the door, his face sweaty. "Good job, sweetheart." Then his eyes skated over to the empty bag of jerky in the passenger seat. "I'll let that slide... this time."

Kat hopped out of the truck and patted him on the chest. "Careful, buddy. Your veiled threats only make me want to see what you're hiding in the glove compartment."

"Gloves."

"Oh? Because I could have sworn I picked up the faint aroma of honey-roasted peanuts."

He gave her a sinister smile, one eyebrow arched. "I bet Prince has his hands full with you."

"Not as much as I do with him," she suggested in a silken voice.

Wheeler barked out a laugh as she handed him the keys and strutted back to Prince's truck. Little did Wheeler know just how true that statement was.

When Prince emerged from the truck, she drew in a deep breath and beamed. Not only did they wind up having an exciting excursion, but lives were saved in the process.

Well, maybe not lives, but a tree counted. Especially when lives might have been lost had the tree never made it home.

Kat wrapped her arms around Prince's neck, and when he stood up straight, her feet were dangling off the ground. Realizing he wasn't going to sweep her up in his arms in front of these men, she locked her legs around his waist, which put a blush on his cheeks.

Prince cleared his throat. "Do you need anything else?" he asked the Cole brothers.

Kat heard them chuckling from behind her. "We'll be sure to let Austin know you helped us out," Denver said. "See ya later, Katarina."

She threw her head back and looked at them upside down. "*Adios, amigos.*"

Their tires crunched on the snow as they drove away, leaving Kat and Prince behind on a secluded country road.

Snow quietly fell around them, and she kissed the flakes off his face as he trudged toward the truck. Then she rubbed her nose against his, starved for affection.

"You're like dating a snowstorm," he said.

"Mmm, I've always wanted to be compared to a weather event." Kat tasted his lips. His reluctance made her even more determined. After all, Prince was a phenomenal kisser if nothing else. "Has anyone ever compared you to an earthquake?" She nibbled his ear and whispered, "Magnitude nine-point-five."

"What happened to the other half point?"

"That's a deduction for not kissing me back."

When they reached the truck, he pinned her against it and delivered a kiss that melted the snow beneath their feet. Prince drew back and wrinkled his nose. "Why do you taste like dog treats?"

Kat laughed and wrapped her arms around his midsection. "How do you know what dog treats taste like? Come on, Charming. Let's go back to your place and snuggle."

CHAPTER 6
Izzy and Jericho

IZZY PUT ON HER BLACK snow boots with the brown fur cuffs. After gathering all the blankets and sheets and placing them downstairs, she changed out of her sleep shorts and into a long grey dress with a slit up the side that went just above the knee. Aside from her red hair, her long legs were her best asset. But it was too damn cold to be parading around in an open dress, so she put on a pair of black leggings she rarely wore. Even with the rooms sealed off, it hadn't taken long for the temperature to drop.

She peered through a window by the front door and admired the contrast between the dark tree trunks and the frosted ground. Snow had a way of making the world appear quieter, reminding its audience how tranquil and elegant Mother Nature could be.

A stampede sounded behind her.

"Boys, quit running in the house."

They could hardly be called boys anymore. Lennon's voice

had been the first to change, and they'd matured so much in just the past year. Her two rambunctious redheads were now assuming the role of protectors—a natural instinct among alpha males. They were always quick to step in and help the family. Izzy knew her sons would one day become a force to be reckoned with, but for now they were still her babies.

"We're helping Uncle Reno," Hendrix said excitedly. Reno and April had thankfully made it back a short time ago. "He's getting out the big grill and wanted us to find Dad's matches."

Izzy bubbled with laughter and turned around. "Can they fit the whole turkey in that thing?"

Lennon chortled. "We'll find out."

"Are you going to help your grandma in the kitchen?"

The boys looked at each other, and Lennon quickly replied, "Aunt Maizy and Uncle Will volunteered."

She smiled and shook her head as they raced each other upstairs. Those two kids never wanted anything to do with cooking. Couldn't blame them—it wasn't exactly in their genes. Izzy wasn't a domesticated woman, and her mate had no problem with that. Jericho appreciated a home-cooked meal like anyone, but he was just as satisfied with eating out for the rest of his life.

Izzy looked out the narrow window. Donuts and hot cocoa would be heavenly on a day like this. Too bad the roads were a mess.

That got her to thinking. It would be dark in an hour.

Denver and Wheeler had been gone a long time. They told Austin they were taking a detour since one of the roads had barricades because of an accident. But that was hours ago. There weren't a whole lot of routes that led to the Weston house, so she only hoped they were taking their time and driving safely. If all else failed, they could shift and make it back to the house in no time flat.

"Mom, I can't find Sparty," Melody said quietly.

Izzy turned around and noticed the worried look on her daughter's freckled face. "He's probably around here somewhere."

Melody tugged on a strand of her wavy hair, the purple twining around her finger. "No, I looked everywhere. And I mean *everywhere*. Aunt Naya searched upstairs."

She cupped Melody's face in her hands. At five nine, Melody was as tall as her mother. She had her father's jade-green eyes and brown hair—when she didn't dye it—and her mother's long legs and freckles. Izzy had always hated her freckles. They were the curse of the redhead, but they were absolutely stunning on Melody. She hadn't quite grown into those pouty lips and long legs, but Jericho would soon have his hands full with suitors. Melody's eyes still shone with innocence, and it was clear she hadn't gone through her first change, which marked adulthood for Shifters. As long as her wolf remained asleep, Melody would remain a child in their eyes.

And that didn't make things any easier. Over the past year,

Jericho had remarked how men were looking at her differently. Izzy had grown up receiving the same kind of attention, and it was how she learned to embrace her sexuality and be confident in her own skin. But Melody was different. She'd always been a tomboy, so now she was not only facing her first shift in the coming years but also dealing with this transitional period where she was becoming a woman. It was obvious she struggled with her looks, and it often made Izzy wonder if she'd screwed her up somehow. Izzy tried to set a good example by holding down a respectable job at the bakery and reminding Melody that she could be more than just somebody's mate.

"Mom, why are you staring at me like that?"

Izzy sighed. "You're just growing up so fast. What happened to my little girl in pigtails?"

Melody played with the white drawstrings on her handmade hoodie shirt. It was a unique patchwork of dark and light greys. "I'm still here. You should have more kids if you miss having a little girl around. I'd like a kid sister. Maybe you'll get the little princess you always dreamed of having."

Izzy pinched Mel's nose. "You *are* my little princess. I need a decade to recover after raising you kids. Plus the thought of another set of twins—"

"That isn't hereditary, is it?"

Izzy put her arm around Mel and walked toward the kitchen. "I think it skips every other generation."

"It didn't skip Uncle Ben and Wheeler's generation."

"Well, look at it this way. You'll kill two birds with one stone. Don't worry about Sparty. We've got bigger problems to contend with, and cats are clever. Did Uncle Reno give you something to do?"

"No. Can I search outside around the house while there's still light? He's probably hiding under a car or something."

Izzy knew what it felt like to have nothing important to do in a time of crisis. It was what kept your mind distracted and made you feel like you were contributing. "Fine. But put your coat on and don't wander far. It's getting dark soon."

"Thanks, Mom!" Melody turned on her heel and hustled toward the front door.

Kids. Sometimes Izzy wondered how it all happened. One minute she was a drifter working in bars as a waitress, and the next she was anchored to a man who worshipped her and was the mother of three rambunctious children.

Izzy ambled into the kitchen and gave Lynn a hug from behind. Lynn's blond hair smelled like dye, and it looked like she'd recently touched up her roots. "You should sit down and rest."

"That's what I keep telling her," Maddox complained in his slow Southern drawl. "She thinks I'm badgering her, so I'll just sit here at the table and work my puzzle like a damn fool."

Izzy snorted and turned her gaze to the long table. Maddox didn't have on his favorite brown hat, so his shoulder-length hair hung around his face as he stared down at his puzzle pieces.

"Maybe you should ask nicely," Izzy suggested.

"She doesn't listen to a thing I say, no matter how much sugar I put on it."

"I've got a million things to do," Lynn said with a harried look on her face. "Christmas dinner is *ruined*."

Izzy spoke calmly, knowing how much planning Lynn had put into this. "Reno's setting up the grill. It's going to be fabulous. You know how a grill makes everything taste even better, so don't worry. It's all gravy. Is there anything I can help you with before I check on Jericho?"

"No, hon. Maizy and William helped me prepare a few cold dishes, but I don't think we can cook dressing on a grill."

"Problem solved," Austin announced from the hall as he entered the room.

Maddox gaped at the large silver pot in Austin's hands. "What in the world's that for?"

Austin walked briskly across the kitchen and stopped at the back door. "I had this in the storage room at the old house. Pop used to deep-fry a lot, and he left it behind when they moved. We never fooled with it since it was too much trouble to mess with. How much oil do you think we need to fry a turkey?"

Maddox chuckled and stroked his scruffy beard. "You're going to burn the damn house down." He stood up and stepped over the bench. "I've gotta watch this."

"Take that far away from the house," Lynn ordered.

Maddox grabbed his hat from a hook on the wall and put it on. "You got enough oil?"

Austin opened the back door. "Will motor oil work?"

They belted out a laugh and went outside, the door slamming behind them.

Lynn untied her apron in the back. "I hope they were kidding."

Izzy knew better. The Weston pack bought food in large quantities, and that meant bulk-sized everything. Cooking oil included.

Lynn took a seat in Austin's chair at the end of the long table. She tapped her chin with her finger, her eyes skating upward. "If Austin can fry the turkey, that means we'll have the grill for corn. I was going to make mashed potatoes, but maybe I'll just cut those into wedges instead. We'll have to do without homemade bread. I knew I should have bought some of those frozen rolls. The vegetables and dip should stay cold in the fridge, but I don't see how that's enough food to feed everyone. I can't put baked beans on the grill, can I?"

Izzy wasn't sure. Plastic would melt. "Maybe you can put them in a pot or something and cover it with foil?"

Lynn rubbed her temples. "I suppose, but it'll get cold before everything's served. We don't have a stove or warming oven to keep things hot, and nobody wants cold peas or carrots."

Izzy opened the cabinet and took out a bottle of vodka. She

poured some into a short glass and mixed it with orange juice. "Lynn, I think you need to relax and let the men take care of the rest. You deserve a break, and they can handle it from here." She set the glass on the table and looked out through the row of tall windows.

Reno was cleaning the grill while Lexi peered inside the coolers. Izzy was confident everything would work out, even if that meant having a nontraditional meal.

Lynn choked on her drink and set down the glass. "What's in this?"

Izzy gave her a quick hug. "Your reward. Now go lie down by the fire and put your feet up. That's an order."

"You know I don't like alcohol." She pushed the glass away. "I wonder if I can find a way to heat up a kettle of water."

Izzy took the glass and guzzled it down. "I'm not going to leave if you're just going to get back up and start fiddling with things in the kitchen."

Maddox opened the back door and kicked the snow off his boots before coming inside.

Lynn yawned. "You won't have to worry about that, hon. I don't think a bulldozer could move me out of this seat."

Maddox circled around the table and scooped her up in his arms. His hat toppled onto the floor, and Lynn shrieked something along the lines of "Put me down!"

Maddox staggered toward the hall, carrying his woman out of the room. He could be abrasive and rub people in the house the wrong way, but no one could deny his love for Lynn. Though opposites, they were a perfect match. He looked after her, treated her with respect, and didn't seem to give a hoot that she was an aging human.

When Izzy lifted her gaze to the window, Reno and Lexi were gone. So was the grill. Curious, she headed toward the front of the house and stepped onto the porch. Someone had shoveled and swept away the snow from the front door to the bottom of the steps, but a fresh layer was erasing all their hard work.

Reno and Lexi had moved the grill to the front—away from the house and trees and next to a giant snowman wearing a long red scarf. Izzy didn't think the house could catch on fire with all this humidity, but better safe than sorry.

Where the heck is Jericho? He'd gone out to the garage a while ago, but he should have been back by now.

Izzy headed down the steps and trudged across the snow, the air fogging in front of her face with each breath. The house was adorned with lights. They lined the roof and windows, their glass shells empty of brilliant colors. What a shame the pack wouldn't get to enjoy them this year.

When a gust of wind blew, she heard the tiny crackles of snow hitting the windows and skating across the roof. It made her hustle a little faster.

"Jericho?"

"In here," he called out from the garage.

Thanks to Reno's summer project—installing solar-powered garage door openers—they had no trouble accessing the garage during a power outage.

Izzy was moving around Denver's BMW when a light beamed in her eyes. She held up her hand to shield her face. "Don't shine that in my eyes."

"Sorry, baby."

"What are you still doing in here?"

Izzy had to pause and admire how delicious Jericho looked. Southern men didn't think jackets and winter clothes were manly, and Jericho was no different. He had on a black shirt with long sleeves. No coat. No scarf. No gloves. Because it was Christmas, he'd put conditioner in his hair, so it was all soft and sexy. Jericho preferred the grunge look, but Izzy loved gripping that long, lovely hair in the throes of passion.

He set the large rectangular flashlight on the workbench to the right. "I'm looking for my old acoustic guitar. I thought I put it out here, but maybe it's in the storage room by the kitchen."

"Aw." She wrapped her arms around his warm body and looked up at her tall, handsome mate. "Were you going to play music for us?"

He shrugged. "I thought it might be cool since we can't watch TV."

"You smell good," she purred, rubbing up against him.

And just as quick as a match striking a matchbook,

heat ignited between them. He lifted her onto the wooden workbench and kissed her deep, his hand sliding up her thigh and rubbing between her legs.

Izzy moaned and drew back. "We can't. Reno and Austin are out there."

Jericho mashed his lips against hers and held out his right arm. A click sounded from something in his hand, and the garage door began lowering.

The passion between them swelled, and when his fingers lightly grazed that sensitive spot on the back of her neck, she gasped. Jericho gripped the waistband of her leggings and pulled them down with her panties, but the boots hindered their release.

He ducked down and then reappeared between her legs, his mouth devouring her sex, his hot tongue lapping and circling just the way she liked.

Izzy gasped loudly and reached up for something to grab on to, but the only things over her head were tools neatly hanging on a pegboard. A wrench fell, then a set of pliers.

He massaged her thighs while licking and sucking. "You like that, Isabelle?" he asked. "Do you want more?"

She touched his soft hair and melted. "Yes."

Jericho stood up and unzipped his jeans. His green eyes were dark with desire, and his lips parted when she lifted her dress above her hips. "You're even sexier than the day we met."

Between the cold air and the heat of their bodies, Izzy was

experiencing every type of extreme. Jericho freed himself and slowly stroked the head of his shaft against her opening.

"Baby, you're so wet," he whispered.

She shuddered, intoxicated by his scent. "Take off your shirt."

Without hesitation, he followed her command. Izzy feasted her eyes upon his magnificent body. Jericho Sexton Cole was easily six feet four inches of pure charisma. She stroked the tattoo on his left arm as he maintained eye contact, moving closer and thrusting deep inside her.

She cried out when he buried himself to the hilt. "Don't stop." She rubbed her thighs against him and rocked her hips. "Please don't stop."

"Jericho!" Austin yelled from outside the garage.

Jericho flattened his hands on the workbench and pressed a kiss to her neck, just where she liked it. "I'm going to fuck you, Isabelle."

This wasn't going to be sweet and tender but fast and rough. They didn't have time, and someone might catch them.

He thrust his hips in a frenetic motion, and she moaned loudly.

Jericho covered her mouth with his hand. "Shhh, they'll hear us. Put your mouth against my neck and bite down when you feel yourself coming."

Izzy wrapped her arms around his neck, Jericho rocking against her with a pounding rhythm that rivaled any song he'd ever played onstage. Another tool fell off the wall and crashed onto the table.

"Jericho!" Austin called out again.

Jericho pumped harder, and when she felt herself shattering, she bit down hard.

"Ah, *fuck!*" he cried.

The flashlight tipped over, sending a spray of light to the floor. Izzy's orgasm was imminent. She was going into heat soon, and that usually made her more sensitive the week before.

He suddenly stopped and lifted her dress all the way up to her neck and sucked on her nipple.

Trembling with need, she gripped his hair. God, it felt so good with him, so right. It always had.

"Jericho!" Austin bellowed.

"Hurry up," she whispered. "Make me come."

Jericho stood up, his ravenous eyes consuming her body as he pounded in and out of her. Fearing she was about to scream, Izzy bit his neck, sucking and moaning all at once as she came.

Jericho threw her onto her back and climbed halfway on the table as they both reached climax, tools clattering to the floor. A loud noise vibrated against her back when the workbench scooted across the floor. One orgasm after another ripped through her like lightning, and Jericho did that sexy move where he fucked her so slowly that she could savor every inch of him as he came.

Jericho wouldn't stop kissing her neck, and all she could do was lie beneath him, utterly boneless.

Until the garage door began to open.

Izzy had never moved so fast in all her life. Jericho untangled himself from her hold, and she pivoted off the table like an Olympian gymnast and dove behind the front end of the BMW. In a moment of panic, she spotted Jericho's shirt by the tire and snatched it out of view.

"What's up?" Jericho asked coolly.

"Why are you all sweaty?" Austin sounded suspicious.

"I'm trying to find my guitar and shut the door because of the draft."

"Yeah."

There was a long stretch of silence, and Izzy cringed when she heard the sound of what must have been Jericho's zipper. From her position on the floor, all she could see beneath the car were their shoes facing each other.

Austin cleared his throat as he walked away. "Wheeler and Denver are back with the tree. Pull down the decorations from the top shelf."

Izzy glanced up at the plastic bin marked CHRISTMAS.

"If you just so happen to see Izzy, let her know that the twins are helping me out with something."

"Mind if I finish up what I was doing?" Jericho asked, ever the smartass.

"Yeah, you just do that. And pick up those tools."

When the garage door closed, Izzy stood up, her leggings and panties still tangled around her boots.

Jericho eased around the car and gave her a sexy wink. "Ever thought about getting a tattoo?"

She furrowed her brow. "What are you talking about?"

He eased forward and circled his finger right above her sex. "I was thinking mistletoe would look real good here."

Izzy winced and brushed off her behind. "I think I have a screw in my ass."

Jericho cupped her face in his hands and whispered, "Next time."

CHAPTER 7

Ivy and Lorenzo

I VY GAZED OUT THE FRONT window of her and Lorenzo's house, unnerved by the relentless snowfall. "We should leave before dark."

They'd heard that the Weston pack and a few others in the area had lost power as well. Lorenzo's pack was more prepared than most when it came to going off the grid. They had a wood stove in addition to the electric, more than one fireplace, skilled hunters, and packmates with generations of experience living in the woods. Lorenzo had even built an outhouse when he first bought the land, and it was an upscale model they kept maintained. Most of the older Shifters and Natives understood the importance of a self-sustaining pack that didn't rely on the human world. The Coles were also strong, but Ivy used to live in that house, and it wasn't built to withstand freezing temperatures. She imagined them all huddled around the fireplace.

Hope skipped into the room and handed Ivy her leather bag. "Everything's in here. Are you sure it's safe, Mother?"

"We're Shifters. We're born survivors."

It was a message Ivy tried to instill in her teenager time and again. Ivy smoothed her hand down her daughter's long hair. Hope had grown into such a remarkable young lady, but she was deeply troubled. She'd never recovered from the wolf attack, and even though Ivy could see her strong spirit wolf behind those brown eyes, she sensed that Hope was searching for something that family couldn't give her. She tried to be open with her daughter, but children weren't always eager to divulge all their secrets to their parents. Ivy knew that better than anyone. But she had faith that someday Hope would find her way out of the darkness.

"Something could happen to you," Hope continued, worry brimming in her eyes. "What if you get stuck out there?"

"If we get stranded, our wolves will take care of us. The wild is our home. I'm not going to let turbulent weather stop us from doing a good turn."

Most of the Church pack didn't celebrate Christmas, but that wouldn't stop Ivy from extending her warm wishes to the Weston pack at this special time of year. She had created a tradition of her own by taking them food every Christmas Eve.

Ivy drew in a deep breath, the delicious aroma of fresh bread wafting from the bag as she slung it over her shoulder.

Her hands were still sore from kneading and baking bread all morning.

"I want you to listen to Caleb and do as he says while I'm away. We should be back late tonight, long after you've gone to bed."

"What if you're not?"

"Then our wolves will be nestled in a warm spot and will return in the morning. Trust in the fates to look after us."

Lorenzo often remarked that Hope was a carbon copy of her mother, but that's not what Ivy saw when she looked at their daughter. She saw Lorenzo's spirit in those dark eyes, and it warmed her knowing that Hope would someday become a strong woman. She could easily mate with a Packmaster and lead her own pack, but she was still skittish, which was a concern.

Lorenzo strode into the room wearing a fur coat made from the pelts of his enemies. His long hair was tucked inside, and Ivy swelled with pride as she looked upon her mate. He was every bit as worthy a male as any woman could desire. A strong leader, a tender lover, and a patient father. He would always be rough around the edges, but that was the man she fell in love with.

"Is the horse ready?" he asked.

Ivy gripped the steel handle of her cane. "Lakota's bringing him around."

Lorenzo nodded. "He's been helpful around here this winter. I should call his father and thank him."

Ivy smiled and approached Lorenzo. "Maybe it's Lakota you should thank. His father doesn't ask him to come down here to help with home repairs or build a fence. That's something Lakota chooses to do for his stepfather. He looks up to you, Thunder Wolf."

Lorenzo slid his gaze toward Ivy, a twinkle in his dark eyes. He loved it when she called him that.

Ivy and Lorenzo had tried to have more children, though the fates had only blessed them with one. But their lives together had only just begun, and besides, Hope filled every corner of their hearts. Ivy's grown son was like family to the pack—including Lorenzo, whether he wanted to admit it or not. Lorenzo loved Lakota as a son but kept him at arm's length. "What does a boy need with two fathers?" he'd once asked Ivy. Lorenzo didn't think a child could have room in his life for another father figure, but he was wrong.

Ivy touched the end of her long braid and said a silent prayer for a safe journey.

"Mother, could you give this to Melody?" Hope offered Ivy a small package wrapped in silver paper. "I know it's not our tradition, but she's my best friend, and I made this for her."

"Do you think that would honor the spirits?" Lorenzo asked with disdain.

Ivy took the small package and gave Lorenzo a cursory

glance. "I don't think a gift from the heart would offend anyone, least of all our ancestors." She pressed a kiss to Hope's forehead. "Of course I'll give it to her. You're a thoughtful friend, and I know she looks upon you as a sister."

Hope turned a bracelet on her wrist. "It's just that Mel always respects our spiritual days, so it only makes sense that we do the same. Anyhow, maybe it's a silly gift, but I just wanted to give her something."

Hope was a year younger than Mel but a lifetime wiser. Some people were born old souls, and that was Hope. Lorenzo said she reminded him of his grandmother in some ways. She had a long line of Native American blood running through her on both sides, more so on Lorenzo's since Ivy's father was white. Hope kept to their ways and was an intelligent girl who always made good decisions.

Ivy tucked the package inside a small pocket in the lining of her fur coat.

"I don't see why you can't just take the car," Caleb said, swaggering into the room. "We can put some chains on the tires, but hell, this is Texas. We're not exactly going to get buried alive."

Lorenzo patted him on the shoulder. "A horse doesn't break down or run out of gas. Keep an eye on the pack, and make sure you keep the fires burning. These are dangerous times when rogues like to test the boundaries."

Ivy touched Caleb's shoulder. "I have a large kettle in the

kitchen closet. Someone can use that to cook a stew. Make sure the women who are expecting are nourished with a hot meal."

"You got it. I'll have River and Moreland help with keeping the peace. You know how it goes with cabin fever, and I can't be everywhere."

Over the past decade, there had been a crop of pregnancies, especially this year. There were currently three women with child in the pack, and that number made the men especially protective. Before Ivy had moved in, there were hardly any kids, so she knew her presence had a lot to do with the dynamic of the pack changing. Lorenzo still ruled with an iron fist, but Ivy's gentle nature and ability to unite people made the house feel as loved as it was protected.

The door flew open and hit the wall with a thud. A shower of snowflakes swirled in a frenzy before settling on the floor and melting against the warm wood. A few candles snuffed out, and Lakota strode in and took off his beanie. "You better hurry before Trouble changes his mind. He's a stubborn old horse."

Ivy chuckled and nudged Lorenzo. "I know *all* about that."

Lorenzo squared his shoulders. "Woman, you are testing my patience."

Ivy smiled with her eyes. Her mate loved to bellyache, but he would never disrespect her. His love was steadfast and unbreakable, as was hers for him.

Ivy kissed Hope on the cheek. "I want you to do as you're told. We'll be home soon."

"Don't forget to give her my gift."

Ivy turned away to speak with Lakota privately. "Watch over your sister. Make sure she sleeps in a room by the fire." Ivy lowered her voice. "In the same room with the pregnant women."

Ivy had a good pack, but she would never really be able to trust men alone with her daughter. That stemmed from her own experience when a family member and second-in-command had taken advantage of his position. He was a master manipulator, and no one would have suspected him. That kind of violation marks a woman and makes her more protective of her children. Now that Hope was reaching womanhood, Ivy wanted her to be aware of the dangers in the world. A deceitful man and a naïve woman made for a perfect storm.

She searched Lorenzo's eyes, and he seemed to grasp her thoughts. Lorenzo would tear apart the pack if someone laid a finger on his child.

Lorenzo placed a kiss on Hope's forehead. "Go change into your pajamas and put on a long robe. The thickest one you can find. It's going to be cold tonight."

She hurried away and jogged up the stairs.

"And socks!" he yelled out. Lorenzo approached Lakota and Caleb, his voice low. "Do as Ivy ordered. The lack of electricity makes for a lack of good sense. I want the women and children to gather into the closed rooms and sleep together. No men—not even their mates. Assign a handful of wolves to guard the property. I don't want one single woman or child to stray from the group, do you understand?"

"Perfectly," Caleb replied. He bowed his head, blond curls highlighted by the candles flickering in the windowsills.

"Good. If anyone questions your orders, they can speak to me when I return. I don't want this to be the topic of discussion."

No one would ask questions. That much Ivy knew. Lexi's pack didn't have to worry about such things since the men were related. But most packs like Ivy's were a mixture of people from different backgrounds, and larger packs were difficult to watch. It was especially tricky if a child went through their first change while still in their teens. New wolves were looked at in a different light, and the kids weren't yet old enough to move out. Most packs had adopted that tradition years ago since keeping the grown children within the pack often created problems, especially if there was more than one suitor or someone developed feelings that weren't reciprocated.

Lorenzo and Caleb drifted away to speak privately with Moreland, River, and another packmate.

"I can follow behind," Lakota offered.

"Nonsense."

He folded his arms. "Maybe you need to postpone this little tradition if it means putting your lives in danger."

"Our lives are hardly in peril, son. They're only a few miles down the road. I've never seen you children act so silly."

His dark brows sloped over his blue eyes. "I know how to navigate in treacherous weather. Down here, you get one inch of snow and everyone flips out."

Ivy tapped her cane against his leg. "Your parents did a fine job raising such a protective man."

He stepped forward and touched his forehead to hers. "So did you."

Ivy's heart clenched, and her eyes glistened with tears. "My spirit wolf howls for her beloved son."

"Then let me shadow behind you as your protector."

She smiled warmly and pinched his cheeks. "Lorenzo is all the protection I need, Mr. Chubby Cheeks."

His eyes narrowed a little. "Don't call me that."

Ivy chuckled. She sometimes missed her little boy with fat cheeks. Lakota was a man now, but she would always remember him as he once was. She cherished those years. Every photo. Every visit. Every letter sent. Those were the years he belonged to another.

She drew the hood over her head and stepped outside, icy wind chilling her face. The rest of her body was insulated with layers of warm clothing. Lakota had secured a blanket over Trouble's back, and her blue roan didn't look too pleased with getting pulled out of his warm stall. He snorted like a fire-breathing dragon, white smoke blowing from his nostrils.

Lorenzo descended the steps and touched the feather affixed to Trouble's mane. "Does your son believe we won't make it there in one piece?"

Ivy approached the horse and slid her cane through the custom-made loop on the side of her pack. "You should thank your son for blessing our journey with a speedy return."

Lorenzo locked his fingers together to form a step while Ivy mounted the horse. Once astride, she scooted forward to give him room behind her. They rarely used saddles. He took her bag and slung it over his shoulder before mounting. Trouble backed up a few paces, and Lorenzo reached around and held the reins.

After a couple of tongue clicks and a light nudge with his heels, they headed out. What little light there was in the sky was fading fast, and it would be dark by the time they made it to the main road. Ivy was excited for the adventure. She loved going back to the old ways and ditching modern conveniences. It reminded her to enjoy the simple things and appreciate how easy they had it in this day and age.

"Did you bring a flashlight?" she asked. As much as she loved the simple life, a lantern wouldn't have been practical.

"Taken care of," he rumbled from behind.

Goodness, Lorenzo felt warm against her back. He gave her a feeling of protection that no other man could.

"Are you warm, *nashoba?*"

She nestled against him. "Always."

Their conversation seemed more intimate out in the open than it did in the privacy of their own bedroom. This was their wolves' bedroom—the sanctuary of the wild.

They avoided the paved road, having heard rumors of them freezing over with ice. Trouble followed a covered path he'd walked a thousand times that cut through their property and led to the main road. They always kept the trail cleared since people liked to get away from the house on long walks.

"Tell me, Lorenzo. Why do you pretend to dislike Austin and yet always accompany me on these trips?"

His arms tightened around her. "To make sure my woman is safe."

"Horsefeathers."

Lorenzo chuckled. "Fair enough. Local packs should stay united. Now tell me why it is that you show this pack more hospitality than you do our other allies."

"I show them *all* kindness."

"Yes, but you're not dragging your mate out on horseback in a blizzard to knock on Prince's door or even Tristan's. The Coles took you in, but that was long ago."

Ivy removed her hood so she could get a better look at him over her shoulder. "Austin didn't just take me in, he saved me. He could have said no to my father, and most Packmasters wouldn't have taken in a single woman under those circumstances. I knew my father wanted me out, but I refused to go with any packs in the area. The Shifters are wild up there in Oklahoma, and the men in my father's pack were getting too forward with me. I liked Lexi the moment I saw her. I had a good feeling about them."

Trouble bobbed his head a few times and turned to the left.

Ivy rubbed her cold nose and continued. "I could have wound up in the wrong kind of pack, and I would have never met you. Maybe his way is different from ours, but we each have a path to follow. Like Trouble here."

"We may not even be on the path," he pointed out.

She looked up. "Then we'll just have to see where it leads."

They weren't aware that they'd reached the main road until the horse's hooves clip-clopped on the cement where tires had pressed down and melted the snow into long tracks. Lorenzo turned on a powerful flashlight and handed it to Ivy while he held the reins.

"You shine brighter than any winter moon." He placed a kiss against her cheek.

"That's my love for you."

He nestled his chin on her shoulder. "You're bewitching. I never know when your words are true or veiling sarcasm."

"Perhaps I need to be mysterious to keep your interest," she suggested, holding her head high and switching the flashlight to her right hand.

Lorenzo weaved his right arm beneath her coat and cupped his hand between her legs. "Careful, sweet Ivy. You know how that wicked tongue stirs up my wolf."

Trouble nickered and slowed to a stop.

"Now see what you've done?" she said with an impish grin. "He thinks the wolves need time alone."

Lorenzo let go of the reins and reached inside her coat, massaging her breast with eagerness. "Maybe we do."

Ivy captured the moment and enjoyed the feel of her mate's warm hands against her body. Despite his brassy demeanor, Lorenzo was a passionate and giving lover. Not once had he ever made sex between them animalistic or unfeeling. She understood that's what some women desired, but that wasn't what happened naturally between them.

"Lie back," he whispered. "Give in to me."

His hand massaged between her legs and sent a ripple of pleasure through her. She gasped lightly when he kissed her neck, his lips warm against her skin.

In a jarring motion, Trouble jumped forward and knocked them to the ground. Ivy landed in a pile of deep snow with Lorenzo somewhere behind her.

"I think tonight we should offer Cole some horse stew," he grumbled.

She wiped the snow off her cheek, her hip sore from the fall. "That horse has more sense than we do. Help me up."

Lorenzo rose to his feet and offered her his hand. They'd fallen into a ditch where the snow reached his knees.

Ivy turned in a circle to pick up the flashlight when something occurred to her. "The bread!"

Lorenzo whipped his head around. "Crisis averted. It landed over there." He grabbed the strap and slung it over his shoulder.

Once they brushed the snow off their clothes and remounted the horse, they kept focused on the trail and avoided foolish behavior that could impede their journey. The wind burned her face and forced her to look down. Her shoulder ached from holding up the light, but before she could switch hands, Lorenzo took it from her.

"Whoa," he said.

Trouble stopped, and Lorenzo aimed his light up ahead.

"What is it?" she asked nervously.

"Power lines on the road."

She squinted, studying the shapes in the distance. The flashlight only reached so far. There were also two abandoned cars next to the pole. "Are they live wires?"

"I don't know, but we're not going to chance it. We'll have to either turn back or cut through the property."

Pretty flakes drifted quietly around them like pieces of cotton. She noticed the snow in the woods to their right wasn't as heavy since the evergreen trees had caught some of it in their branches.

"We didn't come this far just to turn back. Trouble won't know the way, so you'll have to guide him."

Lorenzo steered the horse toward the tree line and stopped in front of a wide path. Trouble whinnied and backed up a few steps. Ivy wondered why he was hesitating, but the longer she stared into the dark woods, the more she felt herself leaning back against her mate. After a beat, Lorenzo clucked his tongue and they continued walking alongside the road.

"Let's just go around the lines," he said. "I don't want us to get lost in these woods. Evil spirits are afoot."

Ivy gripped Trouble's mane and prepared for a rough journey, but with Lorenzo at her side, all her fears were abated.

CHAPTER 8

Maizy and Denver

MAIZY SPENT ALL DAY HELPING her mom prepare dinner. She watched Travis for a couple of hours and put him down for a nap around the time that Lexi and Reno decided to fire up the grill. She was glad that he'd made it home safely with April, but Denver and Wheeler were still out there somewhere, and that made her sick to her stomach.

Maizy peeked into the dark game room and saw Trevor sitting at the bar on the left side. The lemony smell must have been coming from the two candles in tiny jars on either side of him. Trevor chugged down the last of his soda and then crushed the empty can.

"Trevor, do you mind staying upstairs for a little while longer? I just put Travis down for a nap and want to see if anyone's heard from Denver."

"They're probably in the middle of bumfuck nowhere,

wondering why they didn't just go to Target to look for a plastic tree."

She shook her head. "I wish they had, but you know Denny. He loves supporting the local farmers."

Trevor smirked handsomely and threaded his fingers through his dark hair. "I find that funny coming from a guy who eats processed cheese like it's going out of style."

She leaned on the doorjamb. "Anyhow, do you mind keeping an eye on Travis?"

"Go on. I'll listen for him. Nice shoes, by the way."

She looked down at her big dinosaur feet. Denver had given the slippers to her last Christmas when she told him that all she wanted was something to keep her feet warm. She couldn't complain; they were like little toaster ovens on her feet, and today was the perfect day to break them in.

Maizy shivered and noticed Trevor was wearing William's black coat. "I put little Travis down in my mom's room since she doesn't have windows. It's too noisy downstairs with everyone going in and out of the house. Come downstairs by the fire when he wakes up."

Trevor looked away and stared at one of the candles. "Will do."

"Are you okay? I mean, is everything good between you and Will?"

"Perfect."

Something was bothering Trevor. He hadn't been himself

all day. Each time William handed out an assignment, Trevor would volunteer, but William kept him busy with other things. It was as if Trevor wanted to do everything, and that just wasn't possible.

When she reached the bottom of the stairs, she sat on the fourth step. The first floor was suffused with orange firelight, and she listened to the sound of the logs snapping, the twin boys snickering in the dining room down the hall, and her mom humming "Have Yourself a Merry Little Christmas" from the living room sofa. All the sights, sounds, and smells evoked an intimate feeling—like a blanket of memories wrapping around her. She'd missed out on holidays with the family while living abroad, but at least she'd gotten a chance to see the world. It took leaving home to make her realize what she wanted in life, and it wasn't money or a fancy job.

It was family.

Once Maizy began following her heart, she ended up finding her path. Writing news stories for an online Breed news site not only put her talents to good use but also served the community. She made a difference in their corner of the world, and maybe someday she'd get around to writing that novel she'd always dreamed about. Not for fame, but to show people in the Breed world that anything was possible and they didn't have to bury their dreams simply because they had to live in secret. There were always ways around that.

Pen names, for instance. Or maybe she'd just sell her book exclusively to Breed.

Maizy tapped her dino feet together, her stomach twisting into knots. Denver had been gone a long time, and he hadn't called since telling Austin they were taking a detour. What detour? There were only two routes that led to their land. She'd tried calling and sending messages, but he didn't answer. Wheeler had left his phone in the study, so there was no way to get in touch with them.

The smell of cinnamon filled the room. It reminded her of a costume party many years ago when she'd sat on these steps as a little girl. All she'd wanted was for Denver to sit next to her, but he'd drifted outside to be with the adults. Now she was feeling the same longing all over again, only this time it was mixed with fear. She couldn't imagine a life without her Denny, and horrific thoughts of their truck plunging into a river were flashing through her mind.

What if he hit his head and drowned? A Shifter couldn't heal if they were unconscious, and the water had to be below freezing.

All for a tree.

Tears glittered in her eyes, blurring her vision.

Her head jerked up in surprise when the front door swung open and a bustle of movement drew her attention.

"Nobody's allowed to make fun of my jacket ever again," Denver announced. "Worth every penny." He unzipped his coat and shoved it into a closet. After kicking off his wet shoes, he wiped a few flecks of ice off his bare chest and glanced up at her. "Did you miss me?"

Her lip quivered.

If there was one thing Denver didn't like, it was seeing Maizy cry. His amused expression shifted to concern, and he dusted the snow from his blond hair as he approached the stairs. "What's wrong?"

Her voice cracked when she wrapped her arms around his neck. "You can't swim in an icy lake."

"What the train wreck is going on? Come here, Peanut." He coaxed her to lock her legs around his waist. "I'm not going anywhere, you got that?"

His skin was sticky and warm, and even though he smelled like sweat and sap, she couldn't stop breathing him in, couldn't stop feeling his arms around her.

Wheeler dragged a snowy tree into the living room and then let go of the trunk. "Power still out?" he asked, stripping out of his leather coat and revealing his body art.

Lynn didn't bother sitting up from her spot on the sofa. "Come get warm by the fire."

Austin appeared in the doorway behind Wheeler. "Where the hell have you two been all day?"

Wheeler kicked off his boots. "Long story that requires a bottle of whiskey for me to tell."

Maizy shivered from a gust of wind as the door closed.

"Is someone going to decorate this tree or what?" Wheeler asked. "My job is done."

"I'll take care of it," Austin said. "Find the twins; I need their help with something." He went back outside and shouted for Jericho.

Maizy kissed Denver on the mouth. Nothing in the world compared. Her fingers weaved through his hair in the back, and he nibbled on her bottom lip as they fell into a slow kiss.

"You taste like Christmas cookies," he murmured.

She broke the kiss and hugged him hard. "I love you, Denny. I was so worried something happened."

His arms wrapped around her a little tighter, and he nuzzled against her neck, his voice a whisper. "Calm down; I'm about to shift."

Denver's wolf was fiercely protective of Maizy. He'd been her watchdog for as long as she could remember, and it wasn't uncommon for him to shift when she was afraid or in need of reassurance. A few months ago, Lexi had a grease fire in the kitchen. Maizy helped put it out with the fire extinguisher, but she was so shaken up that when Denver came into the room and saw her in a frenzied state, he shifted instinctively.

Maizy unlocked her ankles and set her feet down on a step. "You're stinky. You need a shower."

He waggled his brows. "True that."

She patted his chest. "Alone."

He slid his gaze downward. "I like your slippers, Peanut."

"It's been cold in here all day. Before I found these slippers in the closet, I was literally shaking."

In a split second, Denver shifted into his wolf. She ran her fingers through his grey-and-white fur as he pressed his body against hers, offering his heat.

After giving his ear a good scratch, she stared him in the eyes. "I'm still going to throw you in the shower."

Jericho made a dramatic entrance as he strutted through the front door with hooded eyes and a devilish smile.

Shirtless.

After unwinding the net from the tree, Wheeler stood up and gave Jericho a scrutinizing glance. "Why do you look all sweaty?"

"I was getting the decorations down."

Wheeler folded his arms when Izzy shuffled in with a guilty look on her face and a wrinkled dress. "That all?"

Jericho shrugged and set down a small box. "Got a problem with it, *compadre?*"

Maizy glanced at the box. "Where are the rest? We have more balls than that."

Jericho gave her a sideways glance. "Izzy broke my balls."

Wheeler rocked with laughter. "That I don't doubt."

Jericho kicked off his shoes. "Don't be an asshat. Someone decided the top shelf was a great place for fragile items, and Izzy pinched my ass when I was pulling them down. Anyhow, don't tell Lynn. She'll be pissed, and—"

"Don't tell Lynn what?" Maizy's mom sat up from the couch and peered over the back at Jericho.

Wheeler grinned darkly and whispered, "Busted."

Jericho scratched the back of his head and gave Lynn a sheepish grin. "Uh, about your Christmas ornaments…"

Lynn rubbed her sleepy eyes. "Never mind that. The boys are untangling the garland and tinsel. That should dress up the tree just fine. I'd make you something hot to drink, but—"

Everyone turned their head at once and looked at the tree.

Jericho stepped back, eyes wide. "What the hell was that?"

Something scurried within the branches. It was a sound you didn't want to hear inside the house. Denver's wolf neared the large tree and poked his nose in the open hole.

Jericho pointed. "Who let that loco wolf in the house? I thought we agreed—"

Maizy clutched her heart when Denver yelped and scurried back, his toenails clicking on the floor.

Maddox rushed into the room. "What the Sam Hill's going on in here?"

Wheeler grabbed the fireplace poker and jabbed it through a gap. A furry creature leapt out, and everyone jumped back as if hot coals were beneath their feet.

Maddox cackled. "Looks like you boys brought home one hell of an angry squirrel."

Denver barked as the brown critter flew over the sofa and ran into the kitchen.

Then they heard Naya scream and a pot clang against the kitchen floor.

"Don't kill it!" April shouted.

The twins howled with laughter, and their footsteps tramped down the hall.

Jericho stepped back when the squirrel raced into the living room, scurried between Wheeler's legs, and shot up the stairs. "Holy shitola!"

Denver's wolf charged up the stairs in hot pursuit with April and the twins close behind.

The front door opened, and Austin kept hold of the doorknob when he stepped inside and noticed the chaos ensuing. "What's going on?"

Maizy hurried to the door and slammed it shut to keep the cold air out. "Squirrel on the loose."

"Too bad Ma's not here," Wheeler remarked. "We'd have a nice stew."

Maizy wrinkled her nose. The Cole brothers grew up on wild game, and every time their parents came down to visit, Maizy and Lexi would poke at the stew, wondering what kind of mystery meat was really in there.

Maizy drew back the curtain to look outside, forgetting that Ben had put foam on the main windows. "Did Reno get the grill started?"

Austin grabbed a knit hat hanging on one of the key hooks and put it on his wet hair. "Yep. Ben! Get your ass in here."

A moment later, Ben cruised into the room from the back hall. Unlike Wheeler, he was clean-cut with a smooth shave. No beard, no tattoos, and no dark sense of humor. Ben was a funny guy, just in a different way. "What's the hullabaloo?"

"Put on your coat," Austin said. "And grab all the tinfoil you can find. Reno's heating up the food, so we need something to wrap everything in before we pack it in the coolers. They should stay hot in there."

Ben brushed back his brown hair and gave it some thought. "I can line the inside of the coolers if that'll help insulate everything."

"I have a few thermal bags," Lynn offered. "Let me go find them."

Ben rubbed his nose and crossed the room to pull his jacket out of the closet. "What about the turkey?"

"That won't take long," Austin said. "Less than an hour. We'll do that last. Let's just get the food cooked and back inside. If we seal up the coolers and keep them by the fire, we should be all right."

Maizy wondered if they had enough people to pack and carry everything inside. "Do you need help?"

"No, you stay in here where it's warm. The twins are going to help me set up the deep fryer."

"No can do," Jericho said. "I'm going to have to override your orders on this one, Packmaster. I don't want my boys anywhere near hot grease."

Austin leaned his arm against the wall. "Let me recall who helped you set up the pyrotechnics at your last outdoor show."

Jericho anchored his fists on his hips, and he shook back his long hair, giving Maizy a look at the hickey on his neck. "That was different and you know it. I didn't have them doing the dangerous shit. They can't shift to heal, and no Relic would be able to make it out here if something went wrong."

"As long as you treat them like children, they'll behave like them," Austin countered.

Even though Jericho was their father, Austin mentored the boys. One day they would become Packmasters and form an alliance with the family, and Austin wanted to make sure they were ready for the difficult decisions that lay ahead. Part of that was giving them important jobs and extra responsibility.

William emerged from the study and rubbed the sleep from his eyes. "I volunteer," he said, stretching out his arms. "I've had the boys working all day. Tired kids make mistakes, and I think most of us just want to eat. Wouldn't you agree?"

Jericho and Austin resolved their differences with a glance.

William brushed his curly hair away from his eyes. "Just let me know when you're ready to start so I can put on my flame-retardant jumpsuit."

Maizy swung her gaze upward, listening to the barking and shouting upstairs. "Quiet or you'll wake the baby!" she yelled.

Austin slid his jaw to the side. "My son's up there with a rabid squirrel?" He sighed and hiked up the steps. "If it ain't one thing, it's something else."

CHAPTER 9

Melody

MELODY SEARCHED THE ENTIRE FRONT property all the way down to the road before heading back and circling the creek. Sparty's black coat would be easy to spot against the snowy backdrop, but what she was really hunting for were footprints. When Uncle Reno and Aunt Lexi moved the grill to the front, she decided to search the back of the house.

This was all her fault.

The last thing she wanted to do was confess to her mother and Naya that she was the one who'd let Sparty outside. He'd been running around the house all morning and getting in everyone's way, and when Melody went in the kitchen for an apple, he was meowing at the back door.

She didn't think twice about it. Sure, it was snowing, but no one had given any special orders about keeping the cat inside. He'd been out in snow before. For crying out loud, the cat had gone to war with them. It was only later on when Naya was looking for him that panic set in. After searching the house, it dawned on Melody that she hadn't seen him since letting him out that morning. She couldn't bring herself to tell Naya, and even when Naya had given up, Melody kept searching.

She looked in cabinets, under furniture, and even behind the dryer. Sparty could be a sneaky little devil with his hiding spots.

What if he never came home? What if he'd fallen into the icy creek? Here it was, Christmas, and Melody was overcome with terror and guilt that something had happened to Sparty because of her idiotic choice to let him out.

She even searched the murky pond and poked a stick around. He loved swimming, and her heart sank with every call that went unanswered. She got an idea that he might have crossed the woods to the fort that belonged to her brothers. When she caught sight of a black animal, she ran after it, but it kept weaving out of sight. It hadn't taken long before she'd gone too deep. Her uncle owned hundreds of acres that spilled into neighboring land, and there was no way she could keep searching.

Melody turned back and followed her tracks for a while, but it grew increasingly difficult to find them. The snow made everything look so different, and she couldn't figure out where the bunkers and tree stands were. If she could find them, they could help her get her bearings and provide a temporary shelter to rest.

Now here she was, huddled beside a tree in the dense forest, shielding herself from the blistering cold wind. Nightfall was fast approaching, and she was completely and utterly lost.

Not even her pockets would keep her hands warm. She hadn't dressed for staying out so long in the snow, so all she had to keep warm was her patchwork hoodie and a light jacket. There was a little bit of warmth in the jacket, which had a black torso with down lining, but the knitted sleeves provided no insulation. When the snow began hitting her again, she pulled loose the hood from beneath her jacket and covered her head. It was hard to believe that just four weeks ago they were barbecuing outside, the sun warm and inviting.

Melody grimaced when she tried to swallow. Her throat was sore from calling out for help, but she didn't dare eat the cold snow. Terror sank in when her last cry didn't even sound like her anymore but a feral animal. How long would it take before they noticed she was gone? It was a big house, and they lost track of people all the time, especially with everything that had been going on today.

"Why me?" she whispered.

Feeling an onslaught of tears coming, she picked up her feet and started moving.

"Help!" she croaked. Melody cupped her hands and tried the dove call several times—something they'd used during the pack war. Not even then had she felt this terrified. Nothing was more frightening than facing the unknown alone.

The cold penetrated down to her bones, and she couldn't feel her face anymore.

Now you've really ruined Christmas for everyone, a little voice nagged in her head. *First Sparty, and now everyone will be out looking for you. Dinner will be cold, and you're going to be in big trouble with the Packmaster after your mother gets through with you. What if you die? It happens all the time to kids. You've heard the stories about kids getting lost in the woods. Now they'll have to mourn your death every Christmas.*

She stepped over a fallen branch and lost her footing.

"Ah!"

Her head struck the base of a tree. She touched her temple and looked down at the bright red blood on her fingertips. Not wanting to use her clothes to stanch the bleeding, she pressed a handful of packed snow against the cut. When she realized that snow was soaking through her pants, she quickly stood up and brushed it all off. As if she wasn't cold enough, now her clothes were wet. The air clouded in front of her when colliding with her heated breath.

Why couldn't she have been one of those lucky girls who went through their first change early? Then her wolf could lead her to safety. With her bad luck, she'd probably be in her twenties before it happened.

If she lived that long.

What if no one noticed she was missing until morning?

This is how people die in the woods, you idiot. They let their fears take over.

Melody trudged forward, but without the sun, moon, or stars for navigation, she would end up walking in circles. Uncle Reno had taught her that.

When a marked tree caught her attention, she hurried over and traced her fingers across the smooth etching in the wood, trying to remember the lay of the land. This particular mark indicated a tree stand was fifty paces ahead.

Where am I?

The boys would have found their way home. They spent a lot of time playing in these woods and knew the terrain like the back of their hand.

"Think, Melody. Think."

Not all the stands were the same, so maybe she'd recognize it. Filled with hope, she hurried forward, her legs weak from all the hiking. Virgin snow crunched beneath her boots, and a few birds scattered overhead, sending down a curtain of snow from one of the branches.

"Great. You're going to freeze to death out here and you've never even kissed a boy," she said aloud, then laughed at the direction her thoughts had taken.

Melody wasn't super interested in dating, but she was curious. Lately some of the boys in town had been looking at her differently, some bold enough to ask her out on a date. Most were human, and they were quickly shooed off by her pack. Jericho and Austin had lectured her on the powerful influence female Shifters had on humans, often attracting weak-minded men. But even some of the boys from nearby packs had been flirting with her as of late.

Was it flirting?

Melody didn't really know from personal experience. She could tell when the adults were flirting with each other, but it was an entirely different matter with teenagers, so mostly she ignored them.

Shifters didn't start dating until after their first change anyhow, and while some of her friends had already gone through it, Melody hadn't. Her mother said it might not happen until her twenties. Shifters lived for centuries, so why rush? She had plans for her future, and boys would only be a distraction.

She climbed up a steep hill, her fingers clawing through snow to grip something.

"Here you are on the brink of death, and all you can think about is making out with a boy. Just ignore the fact that your little brothers will be worried sick, and forget that you'll never grow up to run your own business."

When she crested the hill, she took in her surroundings. The trees were spaced farther apart. Some of them were evergreens, so their branches were weighted with snow, leaving the ground below them visible. She hurried toward a familiar live oak and walked around to the other side. Up above, a platform circled around the trunk, but two of the ladder rungs were missing.

Not that she cared.

The last place she needed to be was higher up where the wind would hit her. The platform provided shelter from the falling snow and a dry patch of earth beneath it to sit on.

Melody squatted down and flattened her back against the tree, her arms wrapped tightly around her legs as she tried to ball up and lock in her body heat. It was better to stay in one spot for now. She was losing light fast, and no one would find her if she kept walking in the wrong direction. The last thing she needed to do was tumble down a ditch or hit her head on a rock. She lowered her head inside the open space between her arms. Her breath bounced off her legs and warmed her cheeks.

"Where are you?" she whispered. "I *know* this tree stand."

Reno had built three like this one, each on a live oak tree. But Melody had a sickening feeling that this was the one at the far end of the property line. There was no way to be sure. If only she knew which way was north and south, she could head to the road. But one wrong turn would lead her deeper into the woods.

The isolation and silence made her thoughts drift, and she tried not to think about rogues. Sometimes they wandered across the property line, and one of her uncles would go out there and mark the territory. Wolves weren't supposed to be aggressive toward women or children, but seeing one attack her best friend a few years ago changed her mind about that assumption.

Nope. There was no way she was walking any farther.

Images floated in her mind of everyone gathered around the fire and roasting marshmallows. Uncle Denver was cracking one of his inappropriate jokes while her dad tuned up his guitar. Lennon and Hendrix were digging in the closet for the Clue game to play against Uncle Trevor and William. She smiled, thinking about her mom telling Lexi one of her old stories about when she first met a rock star who changed her life.

Melody transported herself into that room. The smell of cinnamon, a blazing fire in the hearth, a warm blanket over her legs, shadows dancing on the wall, Uncle Ben cracking walnuts, and the protective feeling of her pack all around her. Sparty had somehow found his way home, and after gobbling down a can of tuna, he jumped on Uncle Wheeler's lap and curled up in a ball.

She could almost hear Lynn humming a Christmas carol.

Jolted out of her fantasy, Melody's eyes widened when a twig snapped in the distance and two sharp eyes stared daggers at her from a break in the trees.

CHAPTER 10

Naya and Wheeler

NAYA DREW A HOT BATH in their oversized garden tub. It was luxury personified, with a step to get in and candles all around. Austin had installed it earlier that year as an upgrade, and the women took personal time to soak every chance they got.

She poured more lavender oil in the water, steam rising and dampening her face.

Wheeler came up from behind and took her by the hips. "I don't need any of your scented oils, kitty cat."

Naya swung her bottom from left to right, causing him to moan. Before he got too amorous, she stood up and screwed the cap back on the bottle. "Don't be ridiculous. You smell dreadful. What did you two do out there?"

He stripped out of his pants. "Man's work."

"Mmm." She circled her finger over the panther on his right pec. "It's a shame I missed it."

Naya dropped to her knees and gave him a sultry smile as

she pulled down his black underwear. Wheeler liked her taking control, and whenever she was in one of her dominant moods, he'd be as still as a submissive little kitten. Nothing delighted Naya more than the control he relinquished to her.

She stood up and slowly circled behind him, her fingertips grazing around his midsection.

Naya came face-to-face with the dragon tattoo on his back, and she tasted the ink with her tongue.

Wheeler sucked in a sharp breath and lowered his head. His muscles tensed and contracted as he stood captive in her thrall.

"Be a good boy and get in the tub," she commanded, giving him a playful slap on his firm ass.

Wheeler flashed a wolfish smile before stepping into the tub and submersing himself. She admired every inch of his magnificent body, and he readily took advantage and showed off his assets. Wheeler dunked his head underwater and then sat up, his brown hair slicked back and his lips glistening.

Hot tamale, she thought. *If he keeps that up, I'm going to rub myself all over him like a cat in heat.*

Naya backed up against the sink and drew in her bottom lip. That wild wolf was all hers—scars, tattoos, and all. Her panther grew restless as she admired the way his skin glistened in the candlelight, making it seem as if the artwork was coming alive. It was tempting to get in with him, but there was too much to be done.

He rested his head on the back of the tub, knees bent with his feet propped up on the opposite end. "You take real good care of me."

Naya strutted toward him and sat on the flat edge, a dry sponge in her left hand. She dunked it underwater and began working it gently in circular motions.

Wheeler's eyes hooded, and his lips parted. "What do you want for Christmas, kitty cat?"

She lifted the sponge and squeezed it out before massaging it across his stomach. "You know me better than anyone. I trust your judgment."

Naya couldn't help but notice a flicker in his gaze, one of uncertainty. He must have been having second thoughts over his gift like he did every year. When would he realize he could buy her a bag of trail mix and she'd love it? Naya didn't care about such things. The best part about winter was wrapping herself in his arms on cold nights.

She smiled and took his arm, scrubbing it from shoulder to elbow. "Did you give any thought to my suggestion?"

"Sex?"

"That's never a suggestion. I'm talking about Ben."

He turned his arm to let her scrub the other side. "You mean the vacation?"

"It would be good for you two. Escape this crazy house and see the sights in a camper."

"What's wrong with a plane ticket and a hotel?"

"You've always talked about a vacation with nothing but miles of road and bags of beef jerky," she said with a chuckle. "You know it's not my thing, darling. That's something you should do with your brother."

"Mayhap there's nothing out there I need to see. I've got everything I need right here."

Naya reached across his chest to wash his other side. "There's little here you *haven't* seen," she purred. "Go on and do your male-bonding thing. We can have phone sex every night." She pinched some of his circle beard and kissed the corner of his mouth. "Just imagine what all that time apart will feel like when we're finally together again."

Wheeler stripped her bare with his molten gaze. After a beat, he rested his arms on the rim of the tub, which accentuated the muscles in his arms. "I'll think about it if it makes you happy."

Even though Ben was in the pack again, Naya felt it wasn't enough. He and Wheeler had made amends, but Wheeler was holding back. She wasn't sure why; maybe it was the fear that Ben could slip back into his old ways, or maybe it was just awkward for two siblings who had been on the outs for so long to become best friends. And it wasn't just Wheeler. Ben was also apprehensive, but his issues were different. Perhaps he was afraid that deep down, Wheeler would never forgive him for the sins of his past. Naya was convinced that a road trip—far away from the pack's influence and rules—would be a good reminder of just how strong their relationship was. Would they try to kill each other at some point? Absolutely. But in the end, their unbreakable bond would make them even stronger than before. They needed new memories together that didn't involve the pack.

Plus Naya could use a little alone time. With everyone's work schedule, it was harder to have a getaway with the girls, and sometimes a girl *needed* to get away.

Wheeler reached around and squeezed her hip. "Have you put on weight? Something about you is sexier, and I can't put my finger on it, but it's driving me crazy."

She wrung out the sponge. "And what would you do if I suddenly gained fifty pounds?"

He lunged at her, pulling her into the tub with him. Water splashed over the rim as she settled on top of him. "Want to know what I'd do if you gained weight? Slip off those panties and I'll show you."

Naya gripped his shoulders and whispered in his ear. "I'm not wearing any."

His tongue swiped between her breasts through the keyhole opening in her red shirt, his eyes dark with desire.

She rocked her hips against his hard erection. "You're a naughty boy. Dinner will be ready soon, so finish up."

He groaned in protest when she carefully stepped out of the tub.

Naya placed a dry towel beside him and jutted her hip. "Stop that growling. You sound like the Big Bad Wolf."

He arched a brow. "Maybe I am, because I sure feel like eating you."

"You're the Big *Dirty* Wolf. Hurry up. We have to get ready for dinner."

When he dunked his head underwater, Naya sauntered into the hall and headed toward their bedroom. She'd almost made it when a commotion downstairs drew her away.

"Ben!" Reno shouted. "Go watch the grill."

Naya jogged down the steps. "Darling, you'll wake the dead."

The cold air chilled her wet feet, and she paused when what looked like two bears moved in through the front door. Lorenzo stripped out of his heavy coat and heaved it at Austin.

Lexi admonished them with a glance. "You shouldn't have come. Not in this weather. It's dark as sin out there. Believe me, we would have understood."

"Nonsense," Ivy replied. "We've come all this way, so there's nothing more to discuss."

"Stay for dinner?"

Ivy handed her an oversized bag. "We brought plenty of fresh bread. If we're lucky, it might still be warm."

"Hand that to me," Lynn said. "You're such a sweetheart for baking this for us. I'll put it by the fire while you two get settled."

Naya came down the rest of the stairs, leaving behind a trail of wet footprints that William quickly noticed.

"What happened to you?" he asked.

"Wheeler got me wet."

He smirked. "Indeed."

Lorenzo strode toward the fireplace while Austin hung up his monstrosity of a coat. "Three miles south, the power lines are down. We had to take a difficult route. Do you have any hay for my horse?"

Austin snapped his fingers. "Reno, go move the cars out of the garage and put the horse in there."

Reno barked out a laugh while he covered his head with a red baseball cap. "He better not shit on that floor. I spent all day yesterday cleaning up the oil stains and organizing. And we don't have hay," he said, grabbing the doorknob and heading out.

"I know where to get some!" Lennon shouted, running after him.

Travis was contentedly watching all the action from Trevor's arms, a smile hovering on his lips. He still looked a little sleepy, as if he'd just woken up from a nap.

Naya took Ivy's hand. "Come by the fire and get warm."

Ivy followed behind her. "You look like you need to be wrung out."

"I *feel* wrung out from all the work we've been doing today." Naya took her coat and set it down near the fire to dry. When Ivy sat on the hearth with Lorenzo behind her, Naya handed her a flannel blanket to wrap around her shoulders.

"Beautiful tree," Ivy said.

Naya admired the tree in the left-hand corner by the staircase. Someone had adorned it with simple ornaments, but it still looked unfinished. It was much larger than the plastic one they'd previously owned.

Lorenzo gave Austin a tight grin. "It looks a little naked, Cole."

Hendrix, who was sitting by the TV, stood up with a bunch of popcorn strung on a thread. "We're taking care of it."

"Where did you get that?" Jericho asked. "If that's your mother's popcorn, she's going to eat the tree if she shifts."

Hendrix cackled and sat back down on the floor, continuing with his project.

Izzy glided into the room with two mugs and handed them to their guests. "There was hot water left over in the kettle. It's just cocoa, but I can make coffee if you'd rather have that instead. Ben found an old camping burner that runs on gas, so at least now we can have hot drinks. Our hot-water tank went cold hours ago."

Lorenzo nodded appreciatively and drank the cocoa right away.

"That's so kind of you," Ivy said. After a long sip, she set down her mug and reached into her coat pocket. "Hope sent a gift for Melody. May I give this to her now?"

"Of course," Izzy said. "Mel! Come down here for a minute." She headed toward the stairs and yelled again.

Maizy was sitting on the sofa with Denver's wolf pressed against her legs. Austin said something to her privately, and after a moment, she quickly got up and led Denver out of the room. It wasn't respectful to have wolves lying around the house when there were guests present.

A heavy knock sounded at the front door, and everyone turned to look.

Austin moved through the room like a torpedo. No one in the Weston pack knocked to come in, and Naya couldn't imagine who would have traveled all this way. When he opened the door, a tall figure filled the doorway. Lennon weaved around them from outside, tossed his coat over a chair, and collapsed on the floor next to Hendrix. They started snickering about something, the way young boys do, but Naya kept her eyes on the visitor. Austin lingered in the shadows a moment longer before closing the door and escorting someone into the room.

Ivy sprang to her feet. "Lakota!"

He pulled off his black beanie and showered the floor with snow.

Ivy's face was fraught with worry. "I told you not to come. Why didn't you listen—"

"Mother, let's not cause a scene. I'm here now." He wrapped his arms around her. "I only planned to follow for a mile, but I saw the accident on the road a few miles back. You fell off your horse, didn't you? Are you okay?"

She stepped back, her voice calmer and her cheeks flushed. "I'm fine. The horse just got a little spooked."

Naya collected his wet hat and hung it on the drying rod affixed above the fireplace. She couldn't help but notice how much Lakota had grown into a man since the last time she'd seen him. He must have all the girls in a tizzy.

Lakota stretched out his arms and grinned. "Since when does Texas get this much snow? You must have pissed off the spirits." He combed his fingers through his shoulder-length hair, the ends tangled and dripping with ice.

"Did you come by car or horse?" Austin asked.

"I handed my mare off to your beta. He's out there shoveling manure and cursing." Lakota's smile waned. "I fed her well before we left, so all she needs is water. There are several pounds of carrots in my pack for a treat, but she'll paw through the snow if she's hungry enough in the morning."

Wheeler trotted down the stairs, looking delicious in a clean muscle shirt and black pants. Naya crossed the room and curled up against him. He smelled like exotic oils, and she could tell he was in a snuggling mood by the way he curved his arm around her waist and tucked her against him.

Maizy and Denver returned from the kitchen, Denver finally in human form. All he had on was one of Lexi's white aprons. He saluted Lorenzo with two fingers and strode through the room, his bare ass out for all the world to see.

Izzy bumped into him as she hurried downstairs. She

looked around frantically. "I can't find Melody. Has anyone seen her?"

The twins stood up with alarm in their eyes. "What's wrong?"

"Have you seen your sister?"

They looked at each other and shook their heads.

It was then that a grim silence hung in the air. It was easy to lose track of people with so many coming and going, but it was unlike Melody to separate herself from the group for long.

"I need everyone's attention!" Austin boomed. "If you're not in this room, get in here *now*."

Several packmates appeared from all directions. Ben and Reno were the only ones unaccounted for since they were still outside.

Izzy was shaking so hard that Jericho wrapped his arms around her. She pushed back and shouted, "Melody!"

The silence sent her even deeper into panic.

Jericho paced, his fingers steepled and covering his mouth. "How could this happen? Mel wouldn't just take off," he said, genuinely shocked.

"Who saw her last and when?" Austin asked.

Naya shook her head, trying to recall. "This afternoon she helped me search for the cat. But when he didn't turn up, I told her to forget about it and go back to enjoying her day. That's the last time I saw her."

Maizy rushed toward the room that led to the heat house.

"Oh my God," Izzy breathed. "The cat."

Jericho gripped her shoulders. "What is it?"

"She wanted to go outside to look for him, and I told her yes. That was hours ago!"

"I saw her walking down to the creek," Lexi said.

Everyone knew how dangerous snow could be for Shifters. It erased territorial markings their wolves routinely made. Not only could rogues accidentally wander onto the territory, but so could neighboring packs.

Maizy reappeared, out of breath. "She's not in the heat house. I just checked."

The twins ran for the door.

"Boys!" Jericho shouted. "Stay inside. I don't want you separating from the pack."

"But Dad, we can't just—"

"You heard me." Jericho gripped the bear claw on his necklace. "I'm not losing any more kids."

Austin rubbed the back of his neck. "It's too dangerous out there to have everyone gone. There's no moonlight, and the snow makes it difficult to navigate. *Dammit.*"

The last thing they needed to do was abandon the house after dark.

Lorenzo stood quietly, scrutinizing Austin with a judgmental gaze. Naya wanted to give him a good smack because the man was always seeking any opportunity to find fault in Austin, even though they were allies. Men were silly when it came to old grudges, and theirs went back to high school. But Austin knew exactly what he was doing, and keeping his pack safe was top priority.

Lakota reached for his hat and put it on. "I'll bring her home safe."

Austin peeled off his shirt. "Tell Reno he's in charge. I'll search the property by the creek; Jericho, you take the front. Then we'll work our way to the back if we don't find anything. Keep the porch lit, and gather up some lanterns and flashlights to spread around the property. Maybe she's close and can't see the house." He turned to the twins. "I want you boys on the second floor manning the windows. You've got a good view up there, so take flashlights and shout if you see anything."

Like lightning, they tore up the stairs.

"I'll search the back," Lakota said, inviting no argument as Ivy gave him a concerned look.

"That's a lot of territory to cover." Austin took his baby boy from Trevor's arms and kissed his cheek before handing him to Lexi.

"I'll check out the west side," William volunteered. "Then we can all wrap around to the back. Lakota will have a head start on us, so he'll need to mark the territory if he finds her trail."

Lakota shook his head. "I'm not shifting unless it's necessary. I can cover more ground on horseback, and I don't want my wolf taking over. I come from a long line of trackers," he said, looking at Lorenzo.

Naya couldn't help but notice Lorenzo's proud expression. Lakota wasn't his son by blood, but in that moment, it was clear that he looked up to Lorenzo as a father.

"I'm going with you," Izzy insisted. "I can't just sit here while my baby is out in the cold."

Austin spoke, his voice reassuring. "Your boys need their mother. You're the only one who can keep them from running off into this mess."

She rubbed the scars on her wrist. "I should have said no. Why didn't I just tell her no?"

"Tell you what you can do. Go outside and check all the cars. She might have gone in there for privacy and fell asleep."

Izzy nodded, but it wasn't likely Melody would have done such a thing. She wasn't a little girl anymore. Austin just wanted Izzy to feel useful.

Naya's stomach did a somersault. Had she not asked Melody to help her look for Sparty, the poor baby wouldn't have gone searching outside.

She approached Izzy and wrapped her arms around her. "Don't you worry your pretty little head. Melody's a smart young lady and is probably inside one of the bunkers staying warm. She's just waiting for us to come get her."

Izzy nodded and wiped her tears away. Everyone knew she was a strong wolf, so seeing her distraught made everyone realize the gravity of the situation. Jericho shifted, then William. Austin opened the front door and let them out while Lexi gave him a kiss and whispered something in his ear. This wasn't just Izzy and Jericho's child; this was the pack's child.

Lakota swaggered up to Izzy and offered a confident smile. "No worries, ma'am. Even if the snow covered her tracks and she hitched a ride to Santa Fe, I won't return without her."

"Promise?"

After a flicker of hesitation, he nodded. "On my word."

CHAPTER 11

Melody

WHEN MELODY RAISED HER HEAD, she was staring into the eyes of a wolf. There was no way to know if she was on his property or he on hers, but by the low growl humming in his throat, he was definitely giving her a warning.

She slowly rose to her feet and searched for a tree with low enough branches to climb. Unfortunately, there weren't any reachable ladder steps on the trunk to hoist herself to safety on the tree stand. The brown wolf peeled back his lips, flashing his sharp fangs and delivering a threat.

If only she had her bow.

She took cautious steps toward a tree next to her, her eyes submissively low. When she reached for the branch, she pulled herself to safety.

Melody remained there for hours.

Now it was pitch-black—darkness like she'd never known,

not a trace of light bouncing off low clouds. Not a single dim star. Not even a sliver of moonlight.

Her legs ached, and she couldn't keep her balance any longer. The bitter cold was making her sleepy, and she realized that sleeping on a branch in the dark wasn't such a swell idea. What if she fell and hit her head? Even though the plan had been to stay put, fear sank in. She hadn't heard any howls or shouting, and if no one came for her, she could die here.

It made her angry. Not just because of foolishly running into the woods after a cat, but mad that she could miss out on all her dreams. She wasn't done with life, and there was no way she was ready to die in a tree.

Melody gripped the branch and held on, suspended in the air for a few brief seconds before dropping to the ground.

She had to keep moving to circulate the blood and stay warm, but she was too weary. All she wanted was one drop of light to make her feel safe for just a moment. After kicking the snow and creating a place to sit, she crouched down and cupped her hands in front of her mouth, blowing a heated breath into them while devising a plan.

Maybe her pack *was* searching, and she'd missed their calls because of the wind. Melody made the sound of a dove's cry, this one a long note that hung in the air.

Wood split up ahead, and her heart leapt out of her chest. Was that light?

She clenched her hands into fists but found herself unable

to stand. Cresting the hill in the distance, the shape of a horse came into view. She heard him struggling to climb, and a sharp beam of light sprayed the trees above before falling to the ground and giving her only a silhouette of a rider with semi-long hair.

"Dad?" she yelled out.

Her dad didn't have a horse, but no one else in the family except Maddox had long hair.

The rider slung his leg over and dismounted. She squinted when he dropped the flashlight in the snow and stalked toward her. Melody froze in panic—she had no weapons to protect her.

The horse snorted and whinnied, pawing at the ground with his hoof.

She remained in a crouching position, unable to move and hoping in vain that maybe he didn't see her. The stranger crouched down and secured her hood over her head.

"I knew it was you when I saw that purple hair," a familiar voice said.

Her eyes watered as she tried to focus on the face in front of her. "Lakota?"

The wind whistled against the trees, snowflakes swirling all around them as if they were trapped inside a snow globe. He stood up and took off his black coat. For the first time in what seemed like ages, Melody felt warm when he wrapped the coat around her shoulders. Still crouched on the ground, she tugged at the collar.

Lakota took each of her hands and, one at a time, cupped them in his own. He blew out a hot breath, and the heat burned against her icy fingertips. "You have everyone worried," he said. "Maybe today wasn't the best day for a stroll in the woods."

She kept staring at him, amazed at how different he was from the last time she'd seen him. All the boyishness was gone, replaced by a man. He must be about twenty-two now.

He lifted her chin with the crook of his finger. "Why aren't you saying anything?"

"I'm waiting for you to say something funny," she said through clenched teeth. The shivering and teeth-chattering had ceased, her muscles now locked tight.

Lakota smirked. "Stand up and let's get you home."

"I can't. I'm too cold."

"You will. Now stand up with me. We'll do this together." Lakota took her arm and helped her to her feet. Then he gave her the strangest look—one that put a flutter in her stomach. "You've grown taller since I last saw you." His voice softened as he looked down and studied her features. "How old are you now?"

"S-s-seventeen."

He pulled the coat tight and buttoned up the front. "No, you're not a woman yet. Soon."

"I am too a woman."

He tilted his head to the side. "Oh? And when did you go through your first change?"

She glared up at him. "None of your business."

"That's what I thought." Lakota bent down and looked her in the eyes. She'd always thought his blue eyes were remarkable against his dark features. "I can smell a new wolf, and you haven't gone through your first shift yet. Otherwise you wouldn't be sitting out here shivering. Come on, kiddo. Your chariot awaits."

She wrenched away as they walked toward the horse.

Lakota chuckled quietly. "Still the stubborn girl I remember."

"Why is it when a man refuses someone's help, he's self-assured, but when a woman does the same, she's stubborn?"

"Gender has nothing to do with the words I choose for you, but I know a braying mule when I see one."

Melody reached down and scooped up a handful of snow, then tossed it at his head. It broke into pieces when it hit the side of his face.

Lakota slowly wiped the snow away and folded his arms. "Is that any way to treat your savior? This is the second time I've risked my life for you."

She took a step forward. "That doesn't entitle you to mock me. I'll acknowledge your kindness and courage for finding me, but I won't put up with your callous remarks. What would your mother say? What kind of man did your parents raise?"

With lightning speed, Lakota lifted Melody off the ground and spun her behind him, shielding her with his body.

The horse screamed, rising up on its hind legs before tearing off.

Melody's heart pounded against her chest, and she gripped the back of his shirt. "What is it?"

"A wolf."

"One was stalking me earlier. It's him!"

"Get off this land!" Lakota boomed, authority in his voice. His words didn't hold the same power as an alpha, but there was no questioning his confidence. "You don't want to mess with me."

Melody flattened her hands against his back, still scared. Scared that he might have no choice but to shift, and she'd never met his wolf before.

He might turn on her. Not intentionally, but if he got blood in his mouth, there was always that chance.

After a few nervous beats, she stepped back with the intention of climbing the tree again. If these two wolves fought, the only safe place was out of reach.

Before she could run, Lakota seized her wrist. "Stay near me!" he hissed.

She was panting, her breath fogging the air between them.

When Lakota took a step forward, the brown wolf fled and left deep tracks in the snow.

"Why didn't you tell me about the wolf?" he growled.

"That was hours ago. I thought he left."

Lakota threw his head back and sighed heavily. "Now we don't have a horse."

There was no time to waste. Melody sallied forth. "Then we'll hike the rest of the way. It shouldn't be hard to follow the horse's tracks."

She tried to move fast. She really did. But after descending the hill and walking for ten minutes, her legs were shaking and about to give out. Poor Lakota. He didn't have a coat on, and she had two. When she tried to give his back to him, he refused, saying his sweatshirt was warm enough.

Why did someone as annoying as Lakota have to be so gallant? Even though he was grown now, she still saw the cocky young wolf who always liked to embarrass her. Like the time at a peace party when he dragged her in front of the karaoke machine and tried to get her to sing a duet with him. She sang an entire verse without realizing he'd snuck off and left her alone on the platform. Or when she turned thirteen and he gave her a training bra, which was a joke because she didn't develop until a year later. She was tired of being a little kid in his eyes. It was time he grew up and started treating her like the woman she was.

Melody suddenly tripped over a branch and fell. Instead

of getting up, she used the opportunity to rest. Her muscles were throbbing, her back stiff, and all she wanted to do was soak in a hot tub. Lakota crouched down, and as she braced for another belittling remark, he lifted her in his arms and continued traversing through the dark, snowy woods.

"You can't carry me," she protested.

"But I am. Take the flashlight before I drop it."

She reached around and grabbed the light, shining it on the path ahead. "How did you find me?"

"Your tracks didn't show up until I was already near you, but I noticed what you did to mark your trail."

Melody had broken branches and left markers behind, not only to make sure she wasn't walking in circles, but also in hopes that searchers would notice them.

"What happened to your head?"

She touched the scratch and looked at her fingers. It wasn't bleeding anymore, but she wondered if some of it had dried on her face.

"Damn shame the horse ran off," he said. "I had a nice warm pelt of fur."

She curled up against him. "I didn't mean for this to happen. I was chasing after Naya's cat. I thought I saw him running through the woods, and I kept getting deeper and deeper."

"Did you see tracks?"

Melody gave it some thought. "I don't remember seeing any. I just followed him."

He slanted his eyes downward. "Evil spirits like to play mischievous games in this kind of weather. Sometimes they lure the innocent children into the woods to steal their souls."

She jerked her head back. "Stop telling stories as if I were a child."

He leveled her with his eyes. "I'm dead serious. I listen to the tales passed down from my ancestors. My people didn't make up folklore for entertainment."

"Maybe they fabricated scary stories to keep the children from wandering out alone. Sitting in these woods tonight made me think about what life must have been like all those years ago when people were uncivilized."

Lakota rocked with laughter. "I didn't see any civilized people at the grocery store this morning."

She smiled, but then a veil of sadness fell over her like a shroud. "I've ruined Christmas."

Lakota stopped in his tracks, his strong heart beating against his chest where her shoulder rested. She could feel it all the way through the coat. He was out of breath.

"We need to rest for a minute," he said.

She put her feet on the ground, and when he sat down on a fallen tree trunk, she draped his coat around his shoulders.

"What are you doing? You're the one who has hypothermia," he said.

Melody sat next to him, and he wrapped one side of the coat over her shoulders and pulled her close. She was shaking, tired, sleepy, and not able to think clearly. But despite her miserable condition, at least she wasn't alone anymore. Somehow that made everything tolerable.

Lakota kicked away the snow at their feet. "Why do you dye your hair those crazy colors?"

"Because I'm plain," she said honestly. "Green eyes, brown hair, freckles, no exceptional beauty. The twins lucked out and got my mom's red hair. I know redheads have a reputation, but everyone knows that redheads produce strong alphas. Unlike my father, I can't sing. And I can't play an instrument to save my life. Nothing about me is remarkable, so I color my hair to stand out."

His voice grew distant as he looked away. "You're anything *but* unremarkable."

"You're only saying that because you have to."

He turned to look at her. "I'm saying that because it's true. Someday you'll figure it out, and you'll want nothing to do with me."

She glanced up, a smile playing on her lips. "So nothing will have changed."

He laughed, and Lakota had a nice smile. She used to think he was cute, but now he was in another league. Snowflakes clung to his wet hair, reminding her of the beanies he wore in winter.

"Where's your hat?" she asked.

"One of the trees stole it. Plucked it right off my head." When she didn't laugh, he shined the light in her face and then stood up. Lakota left his coat wrapped around her shoulders. "I don't like the way you look."

"Gee, thanks."

He crouched in front of her. "You need to get warm. This looks like hypothermia for real. Mel, I need you to trust me."

She looked at him apprehensively. "Why?"

"Because I'm going to shift."

Her eyes rounded. "No, you're not! Your wolf will tear me apart."

"No, no. He won't."

"How can you know that? We've never met."

Lakota squinted a little. "We did. Do you remember a couple of years ago when you came over and camped outside with Hope?"

She thought back on that warm summer night when they'd grabbed their sleeping bags and slept beneath the stars, much to the dismay of Lorenzo, who was insistent that some boogeyman was going to snatch them away. "Yes."

"I didn't know you two were back there when my wolf had gone for a run. It was after midnight, so you were already asleep. Your head was poking out of the tent, and my wolf took a sniff."

"How could you remember that if you were in wolf form?"

"Because I walked on the property as a man when I first saw you."

Her cheeks grew warm with embarrassment at the thought of a naked Lakota hanging around their tent.

"I don't know what happened, but the minute I saw your head and my sister's feet exposed like that—with no one in the pack standing guard—my wolf came out. He sat by the tent, and I don't remember what happened after that. He knows your smell, so it's safe."

She shook her head. "It's too risky. My Packmaster would tell me not to."

"We don't have a choice. My wolf can keep you warm, and you know it. You have to trust me." He took his hands in hers. "On my word, he won't hurt you. He protects women and children... even though I'm still not certain which one you are."

The wind picked up the top layer of snow from the ground and blew it around like tiny flecks of glitter. Melody hesitated with her answer.

He cupped her head in his hands. "Do you trust me?"

Melody knew this was a dangerous risk. Her Packmaster had taught her better than that, and to do this alone without her packmates? Anything could go wrong, and she'd have no one to protect her. But if she didn't get warm soon, she was going to fall asleep, and unlike the fairy-tale books, she might not ever wake up.

Melody had to make a choice on her own, one that would either save her life or end it.

"Yes. I trust you."

CHAPTER 12

Austin

A USTIN'S WOLF BURIED HIS NOSE in the snow and drew in a heavy scent that he was certain belonged to a horse. After scoping out the area by the creek, he'd followed Lakota's scent before branching off in another direction. He and his wolf created a mental link with only one goal in mind, and that was to find Melody. Something told him to check out the tree stands and nearest bunker, and it wasn't until he reached the third one that he picked up her scent.

It was strong.

Especially beneath the tree where there wasn't any snow. He stood up on his hind legs, smelling the bark and following her trail to an adjacent tree. His night vision allowed him to see just enough in the dark to make out the footprints. Austin's wolf circled the tree, restless and agitated when the scent of fear burned his nostrils. Then he trotted a few feet away and realized Lakota had also been here. Either he'd found Melody or was hot on her trail.

What Austin didn't like was the foreign scent near the brush, and it wasn't the horse.

An outsider had no business on his territory, so he marked a few spots as a warning. If a wolf so much as poked his head out from behind a bush, Austin was going to tear out his throat.

The scent of the horse and Lakota branched apart. Something must have happened. Lakota would have been astride the horse since going on foot would take too long. Especially as far from the house as they were. Lakota and Melody's scent were equally strong, so they must have been heading back to the house together. For the first time, Austin felt hopeful that this night would end with his pack reunited. Kids were vulnerable, and she'd been out here for too damn long. He couldn't imagine telling Jericho and Izzy that their daughter wasn't coming home alive. It was the grim reality of a Packmaster to encounter unexpected losses in his lifetime, but children were always the toughest to endure. Maybe he'd gotten too confident with a midsize pack, assuming he'd be lucky enough to avoid an unthinkable tragedy. But shit happens.

Dammit, he should've given the pack orders to keep the kids inside. Since they were old enough to know better, it hadn't crossed his mind that they would wander far from the house. Austin had been young once and had done his fair share of stupid stunts, but that was something he'd expect from the twins, not Melody.

Austin spotted a light just ahead. He skulked in the shadows, staying out of sight until he could get close enough to investigate. As he circled around to the left, an image near a fallen tree came into view. It was a large silver wolf curled up in the snow. When Austin caught Melody's scent, he emerged from the thicket of trees and stalked toward the animal.

The wolf growled, and Austin let out a menacing snarl in response, summoning all his alpha power so the animal would know who the fuck he was dealing with.

Austin shifted to human form, the snow melting beneath his feet. A thin layer of steam surrounded him as his body heat collided with the frosty air.

"Melody?"

All he could see was the Shifter's back, and whatever source the light was originating from was on the other side of the wolf. The dark silhouette made it difficult to identify him.

Austin continued his approach, scanning the ground for drops of blood. Some animals sat on top of their prey, and that lit a fire in him. "Melody!"

"Uncle Austin?" a voice whimpered.

He froze. The wolf was in a protective posture; it must have been Lakota. Wolves usually submitted to alphas, but when guarding a child, they were savage and unpredictable.

"Melody, don't move a muscle."

"Easy for you to say. I'm burning up in here. He won't get off me."

Austin's shoulders sagged as if the weight of the world had come off them. At least she was all right. Now he had to get Lakota's wolf to back off so he could find out if Melody was injured.

Austin didn't have time to run back and get help—not if it meant leaving her alone out here with a rogue still on the property.

"Are you hurt?" he called out.

"No, but I'm all wet from lying on the ground. Plus I'm sweating."

He scanned the immediate area. They weren't anywhere near one of the underground bunkers.

A twig snapped in the shadows up ahead—loud enough that Lakota's wolf raised his head and twisted around to look. Austin readied himself to fight to the death as a large shadow drew near. It was larger than a wolf.

"Don't attack," Trevor yelled out. "You'll spook the horse."

Austin circled around Lakota's wolf. Trevor was on horseback, a large pelt of fur wrapped around his shoulders, which he held on to as he dismounted. His bare feet disappeared in the snow.

Austin pointed at the blood streaks on his face. "What happened?"

Trevor gave him a cross look. "I couldn't just sit around the house. There's a dead wolf you're going to have to identify in the morning, and I'm not apologizing for what I did. When I shifted back, I was standing by Lakota's horse. I spotted tracks left by a wolf. It could have been Lakota or one of y'all, but my wolf must have pulled his scent before I shifted back, because I didn't have a shred of doubt we were dealing with a rogue. He was going after Melody, so I took care of him."

Austin patted the side of the horse's neck. "You did good, Trevor. Real good. I'll back you up no matter who he turns out to be. He had no business on our property in the first place. Nobody tracks my family like prey."

The wind blew Trevor's long bangs away from his face, and Austin noticed the light shining in his eyes. Trevor's ruddy cheeks got even redder as he tried to fight a smile. Austin recognized the importance of a moment like this for a packmate, when their Packmaster acknowledged them as a hero. And that was exactly what Trevor was. Had the rogue found them, there was no telling what would have happened.

"Did you find her?" Trevor asked, his breath fogging the air between them.

Austin nodded toward the soft glow surrounding the flashlight. "Lakota's wolf found her first. He's not getting off her either. Mind if I borrow that pelt?"

Trevor handed it over. "I'll head back and tell everyone you're on your way." He shifted to wolf form and took off like a bolt of lightning.

Austin gathered the reins and led the mare toward the wolf. Most horses feared wolves, but those taken in by Shifters were acclimated to them, and it seemed as though Lakota's horse recognized his scent. She approached the two, and after a moment, Lakota's wolf finally stood up.

Melody appeared, her purple hair stuck to her sweaty face. Nothing beat the warmth a wolf could provide. She'd been lying on top of Lakota's black jacket.

Austin didn't like the apprehension in her eyes when she met his gaze. She had nothing to be ashamed of; she was just a kid.

He wrapped Trevor's pelt around her and kissed her forehead. "You're safe, and that's all that matters. You hear me? Now hop onto this horse so we can go home and eat turkey."

Tears streamed down her cheeks. "I'm so sorry."

His heart clenched, and he said a few more reassuring words before giving her a boost onto the horse. She'd learn a hard lesson from this, so there was no point in making her feel even more miserable about the situation.

Austin couldn't walk back in human form, especially without shoes, so he grabbed the flashlight and handed it to his niece. "I'm going to shift back. I want you to follow me. Can you handle riding a horse?"

She looked fraught with worry, and it was obvious she was more concerned about what might happen between Lakota and him if he shifted. "I know how to ride." Her eyes flicked back to Lakota.

Austin shifted to wolf form and approached Lakota's wolf. There was no standoff or confrontation. Both animals knew the gravity of the situation and what was important: getting Melody home.

CHAPTER 13

Lexi

L EXI FILLED RENO'S PLATE WITH a second helping
of fried turkey and grilled potatoes. Regardless of
everything that had gone wrong that day, this Christmas
was abundant with love, magic, and miracles.

"Maybe you should just give him the whole leg," April
quipped, passing the dish to her mate.

Deep lines carved in his cheeks when he shot her a sexy
smile. "The only legs I want are the two I'm getting later
tonight."

Instead of gathering at the kitchen table as they normally
did, the pack decided to eat in the living room by the fire.
After Austin had returned with Melody on horseback, Izzy
and Jericho hugged their only daughter and wept tears of joy.
The twins apologized for not having stayed close by her side
during the day. They even ran upstairs and brought down her
favorite blankets and slippers while Lynn cleaned a scrape on
her forehead.

Once everyone settled down, Melody changed into her pajamas and curled up by the fire near the tree. She said little as she watched her family with a gentle smile on her face. Lexi couldn't help but notice she seemed older somehow. Not one person asked what had happened or scolded her. Those questions would come later, but for now, the pack let her know how important she was—how loved.

William handed Melody a cup of cocoa with tiny marshmallows floating on top before he sat down in one of the chairs. He glared down at Lakota's wolf, who was lying beneath the tree amid a few scattered presents. "Is he going to stay like that all night?"

Ivy set down her roll. "If it bothers you to have my son's wolf in your home, I'll gladly take my meal out to the garage with him and finish."

Austin barked out a laugh. "Don't be ridiculous. Lakota saved her life, and we're in his debt. Someone give him another piece of that turkey."

Trevor ripped off a strip of dark meat and tossed it on the floor. Lakota's wolf stretched out his long neck and gobbled it up. He mostly stayed out of the way, and Lexi didn't mind having him around at all.

Because they didn't have as much food as they normally would, everyone filled their plates with small portions, mindful of those around them. Despite the ravenous look in their eyes, the men ate less and made sure the women had their fill. Few things aroused a Shifter more than going hungry so his mate could have a full belly.

"This bread is delicious," Lexi raved, eagerly taking another slice. "If you ever get tired of furniture restoration, you can sell your bread in my bakery."

Ivy smiled. "Only if your employee bakes it. I don't think I could knead dough all day."

Lexi was pretty damn satisfied with how well everything had turned out. They'd grilled potatoes, corn on the cob, beans, and heated up a ham. Austin's first attempt at deep-frying a turkey was a success. The coleslaw, cheese, cucumber salad, dip, and sodas had stayed chilled in the coolers. Best of all, Austin broke out the malt whiskey and red wine for the adults. Everyone remarked that it was the finest meal they'd had in ages.

There were enough chairs for everyone, but some chose to sit on the floor to help pass the plates around since they'd put the food in the center of the rug.

The hearth glowed, radiating warmth throughout the room, which was already abundant from the love this pack had for each other. Maddox collected the empty plates and bowls and hauled them into the kitchen before Lynn got the notion to do it herself. She was half-asleep on the sofa with April, Reno, and Ben. Opposite them, Jericho and Izzy snuggled up together in the loveseat, and Austin claimed the leather chair to the left. Wheeler and Naya faced the fireplace, lost in each other's arms.

Lorenzo poured himself a glass of whiskey and sat on the floor to the right of Izzy and Jericho, one leg drawn up and bent at the knee. Lakota's wolf was within reach, and every so often, Lorenzo looked down at him with pride.

The fire was getting a little too hot against her back, so Lexi scooted off the hearth and continued watching the twins on her left, who were eagerly trying to solve a metal puzzle ring. Most of the pack was deep in the clutches of a food coma. Blankets covered laps, and the pillows were on standby. Lorenzo and Ivy planned to sleep in one of the spare bedrooms to give the pack privacy.

Ignoring Lakota's wolf, Denver crawled over to the tree. "I think it's time for a few presents."

Maizy opened her eyes from her spot on the floor in front of their mom. "Uh-oh. Something tells me I should be afraid."

Denver tossed a lightweight package to Maizy.

She excitedly tore away the shiny paper. "What the heck?"

Lexi laughed when Maizy held up a T-shirt with mistletoe on the bottom half.

"I may need to borrow that," Naya purred.

Denver crawled back over to his mate and kissed her on the neck. "Santa's bringing your big present in the morning."

"That I don't doubt," Maizy quipped.

Ivy reached in her bag. "That reminds me. Melody, I have a

gift from Hope. I don't see why you should wait until morning to open it." Ivy handed her a small package wrapped in silver, and Lexi leaned closer for a better look.

Melody had her hair tied up in a ponytail, and Lexi could see a shadow of the little girl she once was. Lexi glanced down at her sleeping son and stroked his silky hair. The years were just flying by, and soon she wouldn't be able to hold her baby in her arms anymore. Why couldn't they stop time and live in that moment forever?

Melody tore open the package and held up a bracelet with a small dreamcatcher dangling from one end. "Did she make this herself?"

Ivy nodded.

Melody's lip quivered, tears spilling down her cheeks.

Lexi got on all fours and reached for it. When she turned the bracelet in her hand, there was a tiny metal rectangle affixed. Inscribed on it was *My Sister*.

Melody wiped away her tears. "Tell her how much I love it. Tell her I feel the same."

When her brothers saw it, they frowned. "Jeez, we didn't get you anything that nice," Lennon said, his voice sullen.

Melody crawled over and grabbed each one around the neck, giving them a big hug. "You do stuff for me all the time. I love you knuckleheads."

They hugged her back but quickly withdrew when they

felt all eyes on them. Boys at that age were funny about public displays of affection.

When Sparty sashayed into the room, the kids cracked up laughing. Shortly before Melody's return, they'd discovered Sparty scratching at the back door. No one knew where he had been, and he wasn't talking.

As the cat circled around the living room, everyone chortled. Hanging from his rear end was a long piece of silver tinsel.

Wheeler tilted his head to the side, and his brows drew together. "That cat is hell-bent on ruining Christmas."

Naya lightly slapped him on the chest. "Be nice or else."

He arched a brow. "Or else what? I won't get my present tomorrow?"

"You're not getting one anyhow."

His jaw slackened. "What's that supposed to mean? You didn't get me a gift?"

She wrapped her arms around him and snuggled against his chest. "You'll have to wait nine months to unwrap mine."

Jaws dropped. It took Wheeler a minute to process what she had just said, and when he did, he looked more petrified than a piece of wood.

Ben finally broke the silence and leaned over, gripping Wheeler's knee. "Congratulations, brother. Kiss that woman, or else I will."

A few laughs broke out, and Wheeler laid a kiss on Naya

that could have set the house on fire. Sparty leapt on the couch, head-butting and trilling to steal some of that attention.

This was the perfect moment to surprise everyone! Lexi stood up and dashed into the kitchen. A few candles on the counter provided enough light for her to see, so she opened the dryer and carefully removed three pies—one of them cherry. Over the years, Lexi had learned the hard way the importance of a good hiding spot. Pie wasn't something she made often, but it was a dessert that every last man in the house coveted like the gluttonous fools they were. Since they hated doing laundry, they'd never think to search the dryer. The women in the house were privy to the secret, and Lexi had given them a wink that morning and told them not to do any laundry. She'd tightly wrapped each one in foil to lock in the smell.

After lining them up on a long tray, she put on her galoshes and snuck out the back door with the pies. She didn't want them to have a clue about her hiding spot. Circling around to the front door would throw them off, and maybe next time they'd search outside instead.

Thank God it stopped snowing, she thought. Lexi squinted, the dim flickering from the candles in the windows giving her just enough light to see. Izzy had placed them there during the search, hoping they would help Melody find her way home.

"This was a bad idea, Lexi. Bad, bad," she said, realizing no one had shoveled the snow on the side of the house, and it was getting inside her boots and making her feet slide around.

She climbed up the porch steps, all giddy with excitement, and kicked the toe of her boot against the front door.

When it opened, Austin leaned against the doorjamb. "What are you doing out in the snow, Ladybug?"

"Delivery."

He smiled sexily and waggled his wolfish brows. "Is that so?"

Damn, that lean.

"Austin Cole, you better move your ass outta the way and let me inside before I freeze to death."

He chuckled and stepped aside.

As the door closed, everyone turned around with bemused looks on their faces. Lexi managed to kick off her boots while still holding the heavy tray. She crossed the room, and the sight of three round objects wrapped in foil made the men sit up straight.

"Only one of these is cherry, so you're going to have to fight for it."

Denver narrowed his eyes. "Where did you get those?"

Lexi set them down on the floor and smiled. "Santa. Whoever gets me a clean knife gets the first slice."

Five men shot up from their seats and trampled over each other as they ran toward the kitchen.

That evening, everyone ate pie and shared memories. The room came alive with laughter, and after a while, Jericho broke out his acoustic guitar and played a few Christmas melodies while Ivy and Trevor sang along.

Later that evening, the Christmas lights in the living room came on and twinkled. While Maddox had switched off the main lights and appliances, he'd forgotten about the colorful lights strewn along the banister, over the mantel, and around the windows.

It was magical.

No one turned on a lamp, went to their room, or even made a pot of coffee. The pack remained huddled by the fire, holding on to the magic before it would inevitably fade by morning. Melody crept onto the sofa and fell asleep between her parents. Lakota stayed in wolf form, nibbling on the popcorn strung around the Christmas tree. Travis awoke from a long nap, and they let him open up a small package of plastic animals.

Someone noticed a mysterious envelope with Ben's name on it filled with maps of New Mexico and reservations for an RV rental. At first everyone thought Naya was behind it. But when Ben asked who it was from, Wheeler replied, "Santa. Looks like we're going on a trip." Ben couldn't wipe the grin off his face for the rest of the evening.

Neither could Wheeler with the news of his mate's pregnancy.

In the wee hours of the morning, Lexi fell asleep in Austin's arms—safe, protected, and loved. She woke up once during the night and overheard him having a private conversation with Trevor.

Even though Austin grumbled about Lakota chewing on his tree, and Lorenzo threatened to shift into his wolf and piss on it, the two Packmasters had shared a drink together. Beneath all their competitiveness, they respected each other and would always be allies. Bickering was just a part of that.

Lexi snuggled closer to her little boy. She no longer dwelled on the end of things but on the beginning. The end of childhood was the beginning of a new adventure. The end of winter brought spring. There would always be new beginnings, but that meant learning to let something go.

She looked forward to the years they would share together—the experiences they would have as a family.

The laughter.

The tears.

The changes that would shape them as a pack.

That winter night would live in her memory forever. Their children would eventually become adults, but new babies would come along. No matter how relationships changed over the years, Lexi would always remember the pack as they were that Christmas when the lights went out and the only power burning within their house was love.

Printed by Amazon Italia Logistica S.r.l.
Torrazza Piemonte (TO), Italy